Papercraft

Folded magic. Watched shores. Waiting hearts.

by Brynne Aisling-Rowan

Published by **Woven Moon Press**
For permissions or inquiries, contact:
brynne.aisling.rowan@gmail.com

ISBN: 979-8-9940837-0-3

For those searching for the light after loss.

You are not alone.

PROLOGUE

THESSA

The lake was still, a pane of darkened glass reflecting the stars like fallen embers. Thessa stood at its edge, the cool breath of evening brushing her cheeks and stirring the loose strands of hair that had slipped from her braid.

Her small hands trembled. Not with cold, but with sorrow and anticipation.

Behind her, the grass whispered under her father's steps. He didn't speak at first. He didn't need to. His presence had always been more of a shelter than his words. Tonight, especially, she was grateful for that.

He sat beside her in the grass, setting down a square of thin parchment between them.

"Do you know," he said, his voice soft and steady, "why we fold boats for those we've lost?"

She shook her head, barely.

"It's not to carry them away," he murmured as he carefully creased the edge of the paper. "It's to carry part of us, the love and sadness we don't know where to put anymore. That way, it doesn't have to stay trapped inside."

Thessa watched his weathered fingers work the paper with quiet precision. His hands were callused from hard work and stained with ink from years of writing blessings. She had always thought they looked like trees—strong, worn, and steady.

When the boat was finished, he held out a fresh sheet of paper to her.

"You fold the next."

She hesitated. Her small hands weren't as sure, her lines not as neat. But he waited without pressure, his presence warm and wide beside her. So, she folded. Awkwardly, painstakingly. Each crease a whisper of goodbye to the mother who had been her light. She didn't have the words to speak aloud.

When she was done, her boat was lopsided.

He smiled anyway. "Perfect."

Together, they stepped to the water. She knelt and set her little boat into the shallows. It rocked for a moment, as if uncertain, then steadied and began to drift.

She reached for her father's hand.

"I miss her so much. Why did she have to get sick?"

"I miss her too," he said. "Loss is a part of life we can't control, but this is how we remember with grace. She wouldn't want us to lose ourselves to the sadness."

They stood side by side as the paper boats caught the soft current and sailed toward the horizon—two fragile offerings carrying love into the wide, waiting dark.

CHAPTER I

THESSA

The sun had barely peeked over the horizon when Thessa extinguished the lighthouse lantern. The wick was still warm beneath her fingers as she trimmed the charred edge and polished the glass until it gleamed. A keeper's first duty was always to the lantern, making sure the salt and soot never shortened the light's reach.

It was early but the ache in her joints had woken her from sleep, and she'd learned not to ignore such things. The stiff breeze off the cliffs wasn't kind to joints like hers, but she'd never asked the sea to be kind. Only constant.

And in that, it had never failed her. It didn't judge. It didn't pity. It just rolled in and out every single day.

The lighthouse stood at the edge of the world—or so it seemed to the few who found their way there. Those from the inland villages spoke of it with a mix of respect and unease, as if it kept watch over something too old, too strange. Thessa supposed it did. There was a kind of solitude here that blurred the line between the living and the remembered.

Inside, the tower smelled of salt, ink, and old paper. The long wooden worktable that spanned the main room was scattered with small, folded shapes. Boats and butterflies, cranes and lanterns. Each was a vessel of meaning, a thought pressed into form.

Her father had taught her the fold patterns, but she had added her own over the years. This wasn't the work of a keeper but the calling of her magic, born from intention and feeling. The folds carried messages of hope, grief, or remembrance. Small vessels meant to steady the heart, not alter the world.

Her hands could do little in the physical sense beyond tending the lantern's light, but her paper creations offered a comfort she had once needed herself. She had learned their quiet power after her mother's passing.

The sea was a sleeping giant this morning. Gentle, rhythmic waves lapped at the sandy beach. Unaware of the storm that would wake it later in the day. She paused from cleaning the glass windows for a moment to watch the horizon brighten. Once finished, she descended the spiraling stairs to check the oil supply in the storage room at the tower's base.

Completing her morning keeper duties, she started back to her small stone cottage. It was a modest building, but a perk that came with the responsibility of tending the light. The path was narrow, created by the steps of generations of keepers that came before her.

Returning to her cottage, Thessa lit a single candle in the kitchen, not because she needed the light. The eastern windows would soon spill gold across the tiled floor, but because she always did on her father's birthday. A small flame, steady and low. A soft nod to the memory of the man who had taught her so much.

She'd been here for nearly five years. Alone since her father's passing the year before taking this position. It didn't seem possible. And yet her body remembered, not in years, but in the slow creep of stiffness that had settled into her joints long before an age that warranted it.

Her fingers worked at the seal on the tea jar with practiced care, adjusting the motion to spare her knuckles the worst of it. Even here, where no one watched, she moved with small concessions.

It was easier, in some ways, to live alone on the coast where people didn't see her at all.

In the town she'd left behind, they had stopped seeing her as an entire person. She was her craft and she was her condition. Aside from her magic, no one had cared how much she could still do for herself. They meant to be kind, but even kindness can be hurtful when given for the wrong reasons.

Here, the silence saw her whole. Here, the sea didn't care about her pace or the ache in her joints. Here the loneliness seemed easier to bear than the kind that came with feeling unseen and alone in the village where she had once been part of a loving family.

Following a humble breakfast of tea and toast, Thessa settled in at a small desk in the cottage's sitting room. The hearth was small but held a fire large enough to keep the cottage cozy so long as she kept the wood pile stocked.

The keeper life suited her because in good weather it left time for the work she inherited from her parents. Paper magic had passed through her mother's line for generations, but her father had found his own affinity for it after meeting her. She had taught him much, and he then taught Thessa following her mother's passing when she was young.

Now her hands hovered above a square of parchment, already yellowing at the edges. She pressed it flat with the heel of her hand and began.

Crease. Turn. Fold. Pause.

Her joints resisted. The fine tremor in her right thumb reminded her that this would not be a day for complex spells. So, she chose a simple form: a water lantern, its base square, its walls rising like petals.

She dipped her fingers into a small dish of moonwater and sealed her intention into the folds. The moonwater was something her father had added to their craft. He had discovered that water left under a full moon gathered a quiet magic that bound the maker's sincerity to the paper.

The lantern would be finished once the moonwater had fully dried. It would need to go out soon, she didn't know how she knew, but she did. Every year her instincts seemed to grow more certain in their purpose.

Thessa placed the lantern outside on the stone window ledge. Below, the sea frothed at the base of the cliff, waiting. If the lantern was still there at dusk, she would add a small lit candle and release it into the waves.

It was a rhythm, this life. Fold. Offer. Watch. Repeat. Sometimes travelers came, bearing grief or requests, offering coins or names to remember. But more often, she was alone.

She didn't mind.

Usually.

Today, the solitude pressed heavier than usual. Her joints weren't the only thing that ached.

❧ 🕊 ❧

She had just finished brewing a pot of tea, something sharp and herbal for the stiffness, when she heard a small rustling sound at the door.

Thessa peered out the narrow kitchen window and saw a whistlekin, a small, light brown creature with a ribboned tail tipped in mossy green that swayed like a gentle breeze. It was easy to mistake a whistlekin for a squirrel at first glance. However, they carried a mischievous glint in their eyes, a magical sense of timing, and those small differences in coloring that made it blend into both the woods and grassy fields.

Some claimed they originally carried the wild magic that threaded through roots and stones in the woods. Thessa suspected they had started carrying human magic because they liked to meddle and enjoyed creating a little chaos wherever they went. They would play little tricks here and there to amuse themselves; a misplaced item, a gate left open, a ruffled chicken.

Today's little visitor was running toward the grove, carrying the folded paper lantern she had set on the window ledge earlier. It seemed she would not be visiting the sea this evening for a release. Instead, one of the little land messengers would be carrying her magical creation to its intended recipient.

The creature paused at the edge of the trees and looked back at her with warm brown eyes, as if waiting for her acknowledgment.

She opened the door slowly. The wind tugged at her skirts, but a small paper butterfly near her feet rustled but did not fly away.

It wasn't one of hers.

Looking up, she saw the Whistlekin give a brief nod before turning and scurrying back into the grove of trees.

Thessa knelt and lifted the butterfly carefully. The crease work was fine—familiar, in a distant way—and the paper bore a scent she hadn't encountered in years. Ink, ash, and rain.

Inside the folds, faded ink in her father's script were the words: *Grief has many seasons, to each there is their own time.*

CHAPTER 2

THESSA

The butterfly hadn't moved from the shelf where she'd left it three days earlier.

Thessa didn't look at it as she passed. Not directly, though her eyes flicked toward it the way a sailor might glance at a storm cloud on the horizon. Aware. Apprehensive. As if acknowledging it too fully would make it real. She wasn't ready to try and figure out how it had shown up so many years after her father's passing, and on her father's birthday no less.

Instead, she tried to focus on the familiar rhythm of her morning.

The eggs had already been gathered. Three warm brown ovals resting in a linen-lined bowl on the counter, the hens contentedly scratching at the coop door beside her keeper's cottage. The cottage leaned into the wind as always, tucked near the base of the lighthouse where the cliffs relented in a soft incline that gave her access to the weathered beach. It had withstood more than storms in its time. Something about the way it had remained strong in its purpose lent her strength.

She moved through the narrow kitchen with practiced ease, despite the ache in her hands. A pinch of dried petals, a sprig of thyme, a curled edge of lemon balm. Her fingers knew the tins by heart. She dropped them into her tea strainer, then leaned her weight into the old iron hand pump at the sink. It groaned but relented, sputtering water into her dented copper kettle.

While it heated, she sliced a loaf of coarse bread. It was a gift from the woman who had come two nights ago, seeking help for her son so he could sleep without the nightmares of the forging accident that had taken his father. Apparently, the young boy had witnessed the devastating accident and hadn't slept through the night without waking in terror since. The crust was uneven and the interior slightly damp, but Thessa had eaten far worse, especially those first months after her mother's passing. Her father was a treasure trove of skills, but cooking had not been among them.

She toasted it over the coals and ate in silence, the tea floral and sharp on her tongue.

Only once did her gaze stray again to the butterfly. The message left her feeling unsettled. She hated the way it niggled at the back of her mind. She had certainly experienced the way grief shifted and changed over time. So why had this message appeared now, when she had long accepted grief as an occasional visitor instead of a constant companion?

After breakfast, she pulled on her worn boots, grabbed her basket from the peg by the door, and stepped out into the mist-laced morning. The grove of trees just beyond the lighthouse swayed in the wind. A dense thicket of alder, ash, and the occasional pine. Beneath their boughs, wild strawberries grew in mounds of bright red and green, and clumps of sweet woodruff peeked from between stones.

Thessa knelt to gather the sweet berries, her movements steady and deliberate. When she finished, she would harvest a few sprigs of woodruff and perhaps some rowan berries from the small trees that blazed just beyond the shade of the grove.

Dried, they would serve her well in teas and elixirs through the colder months.

But something in the grove felt off today. A stillness beneath the wind that made her pause without knowing why.

A rustle in the brush drew her attention.

Thessa froze mid-reach, her hand hovering above a cluster of the wild berries. It was too heavy to be a whistlekin. The sound hadn't come from the sea or the trees. Too purposeful, too weighted to be the wind.

She straightened slowly, brushing her skirts off as she turned.

A man stood at the far edge of the trees, half-obscured by shifting branches and sea mist.
He wasn't close enough to be a danger. Not yet. Still, he was near enough that she couldn't pretend he was a trick of the light.

His coat was travel worn, hem darkened with road dust and salt, the shoulders lined with creases and stray threads. Not someone from the closest village where she had been raised.

He didn't move, not at first, just stood there in the half-light of the mist as if weighing her, the lighthouse behind her, and whatever path had brought him to this place.

Thessa tightened her grip on the handle of her half-filled basket.

"Are you lost?" she asked, trying to keep her voice even, but not inviting.

The man stepped forward into clearer view. Early thirties, she guessed. Sharp around the edges, like someone sanded down by travel and time. His voice, when it came, was low and controlled.

"No. Just… hoping for shelter since a storm is coming. I was told there was a keeper here."

"There is," she said, narrowing her eyes. "But I don't take in strays."

That earned the ghost of a smile. "I'm not looking to be adopted. Just to rest and wait out the storm. A day or two. I can pay."

She studied him. The cut and color of his coat spoke of military service, too fine for a drifter. The boots were scuffed, but well-made, the sort worn by someone who had once lived a secure, steady life. This heightened her curiosity about how he had found himself on her shore, so far away from, well, everything.

He didn't look at her the way most did. No reverence, no pity. Just calm observation and a touch of curiosity. And something else, something hidden behind the pale flicker of his eyes that looked an awful lot like grief.

She sighed and jerked her chin toward the lighthouse path.

"I have space. It's not much."

"I don't need much," he grinned and it made his entire face soften.

She crossed to him and he followed her without question, steps quiet behind hers as they crossed the rocky slope. The wind carried his scent as he passed. He smelled of pine, rain, and the saltiness of the sea.

Thessa didn't slow. She didn't speak. But her pulse had begun to thread faster beneath her skin. It had been years since she had felt the flutter of attraction, and she wasn't sure she liked it. Routine was reassuring and this was anything but.

Thessa pushed aside her racing thoughts and tried to pay attention to where she set her feet until they were back on the narrow path that led to the cottage, basket in hand.

"I'll carry that," the man said, stepping forward.

She hesitated just for a breath but released the handle.

He took it without comment. His hand brushed hers for only a second, warm and callused.

Thessa spoke without looking at him and started down the path in front of him.

"I'm Thessa Fenwyck."

Catching up to her, the man beside her nodded, matching her pace. "Evran Thorne."

She didn't ask for more, and he didn't offer it.

The walk was short, wind tugging at the hem of her skirt and his coat, which she now noticed had been patched at the shoulder with navy thread just a shade too dark. His hair, a sun-warmed brown, was pulled back at the nape in a loose tie, though strands had escaped in the wind. Beneath the travel-worn coat he wore a simple shirt and close-fitting vest, neither flashy, but well-fitted. Practical. The clothes of someone used to dressing for a task, not a show.

His profile was striking, at least six inches taller than her, high cheekbones, a strong nose, and just enough scruff along his jaw to suggest he'd been too long on the road to bother shaving. Not rugged exactly, but sharp in the way coastal rocks were shaped by time and the elements.

Thessa pushed the door open and let him step inside first.

The keeper's cottage was simple. Just a kitchen, a small sitting room, and two narrow bedrooms. Everything bore signs of use: the well-scrubbed table, the shelf of dried herbs above the fireplace, the dented kettle beside the pump sink.

She took the basket from him and set it on the table, her hands moving automatically through familiar motions — fill the kettle, gather the herbs, reach for the flint. She caught herself then, realizing what she was doing. Tea, of course. Her father's answer to every uncertainty. She let the flint fall back to the shelf, exhaled, and busied herself instead with removing her shawl. Behind her, she could hear him shifting, looking but not touching.

He said nothing, but she knew what he would see: the paper boats resting in the crook of the window, a butterfly folded from old map scraps pinned beside the door, a lantern frame half-formed beside a dish of moonwater. The air carried the faint scent of ink, herbs, and pressed petals.

"This way," she said, leading him through the small side door.

The guest space was no more than a cot against one wall, a low trunk, and a narrow table with a chipped ceramic bowl and pitcher beside it.

"It's plain," she said, brushing hair from her face. "But the roof holds, and it's warmer than the cliffside."

"It's perfect," he said, setting his small satchel on the cot. "Thank you."

His tone was polite. Careful and practiced.

"You're welcome to use any room but mine, and to wander the property," she added. "I won't hover."

He smiled faintly. "I might stretch my legs before settling in, if that's alright."

She nodded and left him to it.

Back in the kitchen, she stood at the sink, washing the berries she had gathered. Through the small window above the basin, she saw him outside. He moved deliberately, tracing the line of the cottage, then turning to study the lighthouse with an expression she couldn't quite read.

Thessa's fingers stilled under the water. She didn't know whether she was reassured or unsettled by the sight of him there — a stranger on her shore, his presence folding itself into the rhythm of her morning as if it had always belonged.

She dried her hands and gathered a stack of half-folded papers from the table — spells-in-progress, shapes waiting for intent. She opened the door to make her way toward the lighthouse tower.

The wind caught them the moment she stepped outside.

Half the stack lifted into the air, fluttering like startled birds. She cursed under her breath and lunged after them, but another hand moved faster, catching two mid-flight and chasing a third as it spiraled toward the rocks.

He met her near the edge of the garden.

"Got them," he said with a smile, holding the pages out carefully.

Their fingers brushed again.

She stilled, surprised by the warmth of the contact and of his smile. By the sudden jolt of something that wasn't quite magic but wasn't nothing either.

She took the papers with a nod. "Thank you."

He nodded back.

Neither of them moved right away.

The wind settled between them like a breath that hadn't quite been released.

CHAPTER 3

EVRAN

The sky had taken on that bruised green-violet hue sailors never ignored.

Evran lingered just outside the garden gate, fingers still tingling from where hers had brushed his. Thessa had already turned away, her attention pulled skyward as she scanned the clouds. She didn't gasp or frown at the approaching storm. Just gave a small nod, like the storm's arrival had confirmed something she already knew as well.

Then she was moving, fast and precise, double-checking the latch of the garden gate, checking the fit of a tarp along the shed wall, pulling shutters closed and securing them. Not frantic. Not performative. Simply efficient.

She looked too delicate for this kind of labor—pale skin, faint freckles, a narrow build—but she moved like someone carved from steadier stuff. Like someone who didn't need a second pair of hands but might know how to use them when offered.

She crouched to tie down a loose canvas flap near the garden bed, movements quick but careful. For just a breath, her hand hovered near her knee—as though confirming it would hold—then she pushed on without breaking pace. The wind caught her wheat-colored braid and tossed it across her shoulder, but she didn't pause to fix it.

Evran watched her for a moment longer, caught himself staring, then stepped forward.
"I can help, if you want."

She glanced up, her expression unreadable for half a breath. Then she gave a short nod toward the shuttered window on the keeper's cottage.

"There's rope in the bin by the door. The west shutter likes to rattle loose when the wind shifts from the sea and when you've finished that please check that the door on the hens' lean-to has both latches fastened, we don't need to be chasing them in the rain."

That was it. No thanks, no instruction, no fuss. Just quiet trust. This woman seemed so steady and confident. He wondered if anything got her flustered.

He moved without hesitation.

By the time he finished securing the shutter and double latching the hens' lean-to, the wind had picked up even more, bending the low trees near the path and sending dry blades of seagrass skittering across the stone walk.

Thessa was at the cottage door, a wooden box of supplies balanced in one arm as she reached up to fasten the upper latch. She tried to hold the box steady while turning the bolt, but her grip slipped. After a pause, she set the box down, exhaled through her nose, and used both hands to close it properly.

It wasn't dramatic. Not clumsy or careless. Just slower than the rest of her movements had been.

Evran said nothing. But he noticed.

The stairs creaked beneath their boots as they climbed — narrow, weatherworn boards that spiraled upward with a steady pitch. Wind whispered through a seam in the stone, bringing with it the scent of sea brine, iron, and old oil.

Thessa moved just ahead of him, box cradled in her arms, braid swaying lightly with each step. Her trousers, worn and practical, hugged her hips and thighs in a way that was far more flattering than she probably intended. He noticed. Of course he noticed. And then immediately felt like a fool for it.

This wasn't the time. He wasn't here for that. She was being kind, and he was cold and tired and not thinking straight. He turned his gaze to the wall, focused on the grain of the stone, the rhythm of the climb. Anything but her.

She didn't look back. Just kept climbing.

The lantern room greeted them with the soft scent of old smoke and brass polish. Rain hadn't started yet, but the wind had grown teeth, rattling faintly against the thick glass panes. Thessa crossed the room without hesitation, setting her supply box on the worktable and tugging the covering from the lamp assembly with the kind of reverence most reserved for church altars.

Evran hung back, unsure whether to offer help or stay out of the way. She clearly had a system, each movement precise: check the oil, polish the lenses, inspect the wicks, double-check the swing of the outer mirror. She wasn't rushing. She didn't need to. The storm might be fast approaching, but she'd already beaten it here.

He stepped a little closer, eyes trailing along the burnished fittings and intricate mechanisms. "How long have you been doing this?"

"Living here?" she asked, her voice low and distracted as she ran a cloth over the lantern's edge. "Five years."

That surprised him. Not the number, exactly, but the weight behind it. This wasn't the sort of place someone passed through. It felt… held. Maintained. Like someone had rooted themselves to it with quiet, deliberate care.

"You must know every creak in the place by now."

She gave a small smile — the first he'd seen that wasn't shadowed by caution. "The lantern gets fussy when the wind shifts too quickly. And the pulley for the hatch needs coaxing if there's salt in the air, and there's always salt in the air."

A pause. Then, with a slightly wider smile: "So yes."

Evran smiled faintly and leaned against the stone arch just inside the doorway, watching her work.

The wind moaned low outside, carrying the first breath of salt-heavy rain. Thessa gave the lens one last careful swipe, then stepped back to survey her work. Satisfied, she set the cloth aside and moved toward the small shelf tucked along the lighthouse wall.

"I keep a kettle up here for long shifts," she said, already reaching for the tin of dried herbs. "Would you like tea?"

He nodded. "That'd be perfect."

She busied herself with the small camp-style burner, her movements sure and practiced. The scent of lemon balm and something faintly peppery began to fill the space.

Evran hesitated, then asked, "So… what made you choose this place?"

She glanced over, eyes narrowed just slightly — not with suspicion, but with careful deliberation.

"I didn't," she said after a moment. "It chose me."

Evran tilted his head, curious but not pressing. "One of those places you just… end up?"

"Something like that." She poured the water, her tone softening. "Sometimes the world offers you an answer before you've figured out the question. I was somewhere that didn't fit anymore. And then this found me."

That made him smile.

She handed him a mug, the warmth seeping through the clay into his fingers. She didn't sit, not quite — just leaned against the worktable, blue eyes steady on his face.

"What about you?" she asked quietly, tilting her head slightly. "What brought you to my lighthouse—besides the storm?"

He huffed a quiet laugh, rubbing the back of his neck. "I wish I had a better answer. Mostly I was… walking."

"Walking?"

He nodded. "Trying to outrun a few things. Didn't realize I'd walked this far until I ended up at your doorstep."

Her brow lifted. "That's quite a storm to be outrunning."

"Yeah," he said, gaze dropping to his mug. "It usually is."

He turned the cup slowly in his hands, then added, "I guess I've been waiting for life to hand me one of those answers. You know—the kind that show up out of nowhere and show you where you belong."

Thessa tilted her head, considering him. The lanternlight glinted off her freckles.

"And did it?" she asked softly. "Give you any answers at all?"

His smile was crooked. "Not yet. But I'm starting to think I've been looking in the wrong places."

The storm pressed against the lighthouse like a living thing, its howls softened by the thick stone walls. The lantern above them hissed gently, casting rhythmic gold pulses that danced across the curved ceiling.

Thessa sat with her back against the wall, knees drawn slightly up, the collar of her oversized sweater tugged close against the draft. A blanket draped around her shoulders, similar to the one she'd quietly handed him shortly after they settled in with their tea.

Evran sat opposite, one boot flat to the floor, elbow resting on a bent knee. The silence between them wasn't strained; it had settled slowly, like something they'd agreed on without speaking. Mutual. Steady.

Then the lantern sputtered. A sudden flicker, then a spitting cough of light.

Thessa moved instantly, setting her mug aside and shifting to rise. She got one leg under her—then faltered. Just the smallest hitch, but he saw it: the way her hand went to the wall, the barely-there clench of her jaw as her knee refused to cooperate.

She didn't curse. Didn't flinch dramatically. Just *breathed*, steady and low, and pushed herself upright with practiced efficiency.

Evran stood too, slower. "Want a hand?"

Her brilliant blue eyes flicked to him—cautious but not offended. She weighed the offer. Then nodded.

"Just steady the base while I adjust the wick," she murmured.

He did as asked, and together they coaxed the lantern back into a steady glow. No fanfare. No dramatics.

When they sat again, there was a quiet shift in the space between them.
Not quite closeness. But no longer the distance of total strangers.

Thessa pulled her blanket a little tighter around her slender frame, fingers fussing with the edge as the lantern's light steadied above them once more. After a moment, she looked over at him.

"Thanks," she said softly. "For the hand."

He gave a quiet nod, watching her from beneath the brim of his mug.

"My joints… act up sometimes," she added, tone light. Not ashamed, not quite casual either. Just… honest. "Comes and goes."

"Glad to lend a hand where I can," he said, voice just as quiet. "Besides, I owe you for the tea."

Her mouth curved — not quite a smile, but close.

And the silence that followed felt warmer still.

The storm had passed after raging most of the night.

Outside the lighthouse, the world glistened with salt and rain, the sky smeared in gray and rose. The sea still murmured its discontent, but the wind had softened, and the worst of it had blown inland.

Thessa extinguished the lantern with practiced care, polished the lens once more, and checked the seals. By the time she turned to gather her things, Evran was already waiting with the box of supplies in his arms.

"You didn't have to…" she started.

He shrugged, gentle. "I know, but I wanted to."

She didn't argue.

They stepped out together into the damp morning hush, boots crunching against the wet path. This time, she didn't walk ahead, and he didn't fall behind. Side by side, they made their way down the winding trail that led to the cottage.

A gust of wind tugged at her braid, and she lifted a hand to fix it. His hand brushed hers — a featherlight touch, brief but not accidental. Neither of them pulled away.

The silence between them wasn't silence at all.

It was soft.

And something new, warm and tentative, flickered between them.

CHAPTER 4

THESSA

The eggs sizzled softly in the pan, their edges curling with golden brown where they met the heat. Thessa tilted the skillet carefully, her wrist stiff from the cold morning air. The ache in her knuckles hadn't faded overnight, only softened around the edges like bruises just beginning to yellow. Sleeping while sitting against the lighthouse wall certainly hadn't helped.

Beside her, Evran sliced root vegetables in silence.

He hadn't asked if she needed help. Just joined her, rolled up his sleeves, and started working with the easy confidence of someone used to making himself useful in strange kitchens. It should've unsettled her. It had been years since she had shared her space and routines with someone. Instead, she found herself matching his pace, adjusting without effort.

That was more unsettling in a completely different way. She wasn't sure if she liked the way he was making her belly flutter. She was just so aware of his presence.

"Bread?" he asked, nodding toward the tin on the shelf.

"Still decent," she said. "If you toast it."

He gave a quiet grunt of acknowledgment and reached for the loaf, setting slices into the cast iron pan with practiced motion. The smell of smoke and thyme thickened between them.

Thessa moved through the rest of the breakfast prep in silence, and he didn't interrupt it. When she reached for the tin of tea leaves, her hand brushed his elbow. Neither of them flinched. Neither stepped away.

She wasn't sure what to make of that.

They ate in near silence at the narrow kitchen table, steam rising from mismatched mugs. The light through the eastern window caught on the edge of her worktable, turning the rough grain gold. Her knees ached from standing too long. She didn't adjust her seat. She didn't want him to see her discomfort. Experience had taught her judgment would soon follow.

Evran ate like someone used to making every bite count. Not fast, not desperate, but with a quiet sense of purpose that you didn't see in those who were always well fed.

He glanced toward the window once, toward the crooked row of herbs and the small, folded butterfly resting on the sill. Its wings were softened with time, edges slightly curled.

"You make all of these?" he asked.

"Most," she said, without looking up.

"Not that one?"

Thessa's hand tightened faintly around her cup. "No."

He seemed to sense her discomfort and he didn't push.

She watched him from beneath her lashes, uncertain whether his question had been idle curiosity or something more.

When they finished eating, she stood to clear the dishes, but he beat her to the stack of plates.

"I'll wash," he said, already carrying them to the basin.

She hesitated, not because she minded, but because it had been years since anyone else had offered.

While he worked the pump handle, she reached for the towel hanging beside the sink, folding the soft fabric between her hands to keep busy.

"So what now?" she asked.

He paused, glanced back at her.

"Now that the storm's passed," she added. "You said you were only resting a day or two."

He turned back to the pump. "I'll keep walking."

"That's not much of a plan."

He shrugged. "It's what I've got."

Thessa leaned against the table, watching him. He worked with that unhurried, capable rhythm she was beginning to recognize, his hands precise and his broad shoulders moving steadily as he rinsed each dish. There was a groundedness to him, something solid and quietly reassuring.

The thought of him walking away from this place tugged at her in a way she hadn't expected.

"There's not much beyond this coast," she said.

"I know."

"You could go inland, just a couple hours away is a small village. Three days east is a larger town, more opportunities. Orchards, a small library, people who bake too much and share it with strangers."

He didn't smile, but something flickered in his posture — a thread of attention, if not interest.

"Or," she said, trying to keep her tone light, "you could stay another day."

He looked up.

She didn't look away.

"The railing by the cliffs needs fixing if you're willing," she said tentatively, looking at him as confidently as she could with her insides quaking.

He tilted his head slightly, watching her.

"I wouldn't want to wear out my welcome."

"You'd have to try harder," she said softly.

He let out a soft laugh. "Alright."

She turned before he could say anything else, reaching for the kettle to busy her hands. His laugh had made her insides heat and she could feel her cheeks flushing with pleasure.

Behind her, the whistle of the pump faded, replaced by the faint clink of dishes and the low murmur of running water. It wasn't silence.

It was something warmer.

Something that felt like room enough to stay.

Thessa sat at her worktable, the morning light softened by a blanket of low gray clouds. The sea beyond the window was silvered and slow-moving, the kind of light that dulled the edges of the world and made something inside her settle.

She pulled a square of paper toward her — thinner than usual, soft with age, pale along the edges where the sun had kissed it through the storeroom window. Not the kind she used for messages or lanterns. This was the sort of paper she reached for when the words hadn't come yet, but the *feeling* had.

Her fingers hovered over it, not in indecision, but in listening.

There was a weight in her chest, not unpleasant, but full. A pressure behind the ribs that came from the unfamiliar presence in her kitchen, the echo of conversation still lingering in the air, and the way her body hadn't tensed when he stood beside her to cook.

It wasn't quite trust. But it wasn't fear either. There was a spark of attraction. Something she hadn't felt in years. Not since she was a teen living in the village. Quiet Bradley Kellan who had sat beside her during lessons and sometimes shared his primer with her.

She smiled just a bit with the memory and pressed the first crease into the paper.

Let this carry openness without demand, she thought, returning her attention to her work. Curiosity without threat. A reaching, not a pull.

Not hope. Not yet. But something that could become it.

Across the room, she sensed movement. The quiet scuff of boots. The rustle of his coat as Evran crossed to stand near the table.

He didn't interrupt right away. Just watched.

Then, softly: "Another butterfly?"

Thessa nodded. "Of a sort."

"What's it for?"

She didn't look up. "To reach," she said. "Gently."

Evran tilted his head. "Do you always know what it's for before you start?"

"Sometimes I know. Other times I just feel a pull to fold, and it comes to me as I work."

He fell quiet again. She could feel his gaze on her hands as they moved. The shape was emerging now — not quite a butterfly, not quite a bird. The wings were longer, the body more tapered, the folds precise but soft. An in-between form for an in-between moment.

"I always thought this kind of magic was… symbolic," Evran said after a moment. "Like carving a name into driftwood. More tradition than spell work."

Thessa's hands didn't falter. "It's only symbolic if the one folding it doesn't mean it."

"You believe it changes something?"

"I believe it *reaches* something. And sometimes, that's more powerful than change."

He leaned a little closer, bracing his hand lightly on the back of the nearest chair. "But what does it *do*?"

Thessa set the paper down for just a breath.

Then: "It reminds someone they're not forgotten. That their healing matters."

Her voice wasn't sharp. It was gentle but firmly anchored in her purpose.

Evran didn't respond. Not right away.

Thessa stood and walked to the window, the finished shape cupped in her palms. The sea breeze had picked up again, tugging gently at the loose strands of her hair.

She breathed into the folded shape — not words, but intent. That was enough.

Then she opened her hands.

The paper lifted on the breeze, catching the air like it had been waiting for it.

A soft *whistle* piped near the window ledge.

A whistlekin appeared. Mossy-furred, bright-eyed, its ribboned tail flicking lightly as it hopped onto the sill. It watched the paper shape sail outward into the gray sky, nose twitching.

Then, with a chirr and a swish of its tail, it vanished down the outer wall, into the flower bed below.

Evran had stepped beside her now, shoulder nearly brushing hers. His voice was quiet. His face pensive.

"That one felt… different."

Thessa didn't take her eyes off the sky.

"It was," she said.

The sea was restless again.

Not with storm, but with something quieter, a stirring in the tide, a pulling beneath the waves. Thessa felt it more than she heard it. Like a thread tugging at the base of her spine. Like her name being spoken too far away to catch.

She'd folded something sharp after Evran left the kitchen.

Not physically sharp—but emotionally tight. A long-winged crane with pinched lines and no softness. She hadn't lit it or marked it. Just folded and set it aside, unsure whether it was meant for sea, wind, or earth.

She didn't know why his words had lingered. He hadn't been cruel. Only cautious. Thoughtful, even. And that should have made it easier.

But it didn't.

Because what he said about folding being symbolic, not magic, had echoed something she'd once feared was true.

What if it's not enough to care? What if no one's listening?

Her father had reassured her that he had seen the power of it many times and reminded her of the boats they had set adrift after her mother's passing. The way their grief had lost its sharpness and they had been able to settle into new routines and rhythms.

She was standing near the back door, her hands wrapped in her shawl, when she felt it.

Not wind. Not sound.

Just a shift.

She turned.

And Selara was there.

Perched on the fencepost beside the path to the cliffs, Selara stood with her long neck lifted and her wings folded close. Her feathers caught the lantern light in pale sea-glass hues, a soft shimmer that seemed to glow from within. The long silk-like plumes at her tail stirred in the breeze, drifting like strands of water.

She watched Thessa—not with curiosity, but with a steady, knowing certainty.

There was something in her beak.

A folded object—no, not folded. Wrapped. Bound in twine, damp around the edges, still smelling of salt.

Thessa moved slowly. Selara didn't flinch.

When she reached out, the tide bird released the object into her hands and took to the air without a sound.

Thessa watched her disappear into the dark—not fading, not vanishing. Just gone.

She looked down.

The bundle was no larger than her palm. She unwrapped it carefully, peeling away the softened twine and damp cloth.

Inside: a strip of embroidered fabric, torn from something well-made. The thread was dark with water, frayed at the edge.

There was also a sliver of wood—polished, etched faintly with the symbol for safe passage. Weather-worn and cracked. A piece of a boat.

Thessa's throat closed.

She'd seen this before. Not this piece, but these *types* of offerings. Selara brought them when the sea held pain too deep for voices.

Someone needed her.

Someone had already been lost and while she couldn't change that, she could send healing comfort.

She stood still for a long moment, bundle cradled in her hand, the wind sliding past her cheeks like breath.

Behind her, she heard movement in the cottage.

Evran's voice, low and curious: "Everything alright?"

She didn't turn.

"No, I need to fold," she said, walking briskly toward the cottage.

That was all.

And she stepped inside—not to rest, but to answer the call of her heart.

CHAPTER 5

THESSA

The soil near the rosemary bed was dry and stubborn, baked hard by a string of windy days. Thessa pressed the tip of her trowel into a crack between the stones, angling carefully to avoid straining her wrist. It was slow work, but honest. The kind of task that tethered her to the present with the weight of simple purpose.

Behind her, Evran muttered something under his breath, followed by the telltale *snap* of a rope gone rebellious.

She glanced over her shoulder. He was bent over the trellis again, sleeves rolled to his elbows, forearms dusted with soil and the occasional scratch. His cloak had been tossed over the fence post, revealing the fitted leather beneath — worn but well-kept. His hair was damp at the temples and caught the morning light like sun-touched oak. Something in the way he moved, precise yet unhurried, made her stomach shift, just slightly. She looked away.

"This knot has opinions," he said. "And none of them are cooperative."

"That's because you're doing it backwards. Loop under, then over. Otherwise, the wind just laughs and pulls it loose again."

"Oh. Right. Wind etiquette," he replied and she swore she could hear a smile in his tone.

She worked another inch of soil free and replied without looking up, "Lighthouse rules."

The scent of thyme and salt mixed in the air between them. Her back ached faintly as she shifted to her other knee. She heard him adjust his footing, and just faintly the quiet exhale he made when the rope finally held.

Then came the sound: *pip-whit!* High and bright, like a whistle carried on the breeze.

Evran straightened. "Was that a kettle?"

"Nope."

"Bird?"

"Nope again."

A flicker of mossy green darted down the wall, tail ribbony and curling, fur like dappled sunlight through the trees. The whistlekin launched itself onto the watering can handle, chirped twice, and tipped the spout just enough to arc a stream of water straight onto Evran's head.

He blinked, dripping. The whistlekin, now perched like a victorious gremlin, let out another hiccupping whistle.

"Did your friend just baptize me?"

Thessa sat back on her heels and chuckled, wiping a dirty hand across her brow. "Possibly a blessing. Possibly a declaration of war. Hard to say with the whistlekins."

Evran squinted up at the creature. "Does he have a name?"

"They probably do, but they don't tell me. I call him Trouble. Actually, I call all the whistlekins Trouble. They serve their purpose, but they are sure to be mischievous while they do it."

Evran laughed. Not a sharp breath or scoff, but a *real* full-bellied laugh — low, full, bright at the edges.

Thessa realized she hadn't heard this laugh before.

And she hadn't expected the way it landed. It felt like sunlight catching in her chest. When he smiled, truly smiled, it transformed him. He was all weathered strength and soft crinkles at the corners of his eyes. Warm in a way she hadn't thought he could be. Would she ever tire of seeing all these new sides of him?

She turned sharply back to the rosemary. The soil needed her attention. Not his hands. Not his arms. *Not that smile.*

Another tug at her braid.

"Trouble," she warned. "Put the pebble down."

The whistlekins rarely obeyed, but the pebble it had stolen clinked harmlessly to the ground.

Evran stepped over and picked it up, brushing it clean before handing it to her without a word. Their fingers didn't quite touch, but the nearness of his presence made the hair at her nape prickle, not with discomfort. Just...awareness.

"Are they always around?" he asked.

"Sometimes more than others," she said. "If I see them a lot it usually means something's stirring."

He looked back toward the stone wall, where the whistlekin had now curled itself into the thyme patch, tail tucked neatly over its nose. "Does it understand you?"

"Better than most people." She paused. "Not in words. In intent. Mood. They *feel* things."

Evran folded his arms, watching the creature with quiet curiosity. "Like that bird?"

Thessa blinked. She didn't realize he had seen the visit from the Selara.

"Sort of," she said. "Whistlekin are land messengers who bring me tokens of need and carry my folds where they're meant to go. The Selara is more like a sea harbinger. She senses urgency — often before the person in need realizes. Once, she even alerted me in time to light the lantern and help a lost fisherman reach the shore. I still sent his family a butterfly of hope that would reach them before he did. He had been lost at sea for three days."

Evran glanced at her. "And they take your magic with them."

She hesitated for just a moment knowing this would probably support his idea that the magic was purely symbolic. "Not the Selara. The sea or the wind make those deliveries. They carry what I make to places I can't go, to places the whistlekins can't reach."

A breeze rolled in from the cliffs. She pressed her palm against the soil again, grounding herself before continuing.

"I used to be part of that world," she said quietly. "Villages. Markets. Paths. But my body stopped cooperating. The pain got worse. My magic got stronger. I felt like I was being seen for what I could or couldn't do. I didn't belong there anymore."

She didn't expect him to respond — not really. Most people tried to fix it, or look away.

Evran's voice was soft. "So you built a way to still help. Just...differently."

That surprised her.

"I suppose," she said.

"And the creatures helped build that bridge."

She looked over at him then — properly — and saw no pity in his expression. Just understanding. Just... *witnessing*.

It was, somehow, worse. And better.

"They're how I stay part of the world," she admitted. "Even when I can't always walk in it."

Evran didn't speak; he just crouched beside her and helped brush soil over the base of the rosemary.

Together, in silence, they made the plant steady again.

Later that night, after the dishes were rinsed and the wind had died down, Thessa sat by the window with her folding box open on her lap.

The lighthouse was still. The only sound was the low, regular churn of waves brushing the shore.

She held a square of paper — soft cream, flecked with gold. A new one. Unused. She wasn't sure yet what it wanted to be.

Usually, she folded with purpose. A lantern for grief. A boat for remembrance. A butterfly for hope and blessings not yet spoken.

But tonight she just folded.

A curve here. A twist there. Her hands knew the shapes even when her mind did not.

When she finished, the paper had taken the shape of a small spiral-winged moth — delicate, quiet, not meant for flight just yet.

She turned it in her hand, watching the shadows play along its edges. And instead of carrying it to the window or tucking it into her basket of offerings, she set it down on the sill.

Not outside. Not released.

Just… waiting.

Maybe tomorrow she'd know what it was for.

Maybe not.

But for tonight, it could stay here.

CHAPTER 6

THESSA

She carefully counted the sheets of paper left in the drawer. Four sheets. Ink was low too. She knew in the cottage her supplies of flour and lamp oil were also running out. Looking out the lighthouse glass, she gazed across the water and tried to steel herself for a trip into town.

The traveling merchant should have come days ago. He hadn't. The silence of the road had pressed on her ever since.

Back in her small cottage, she packed a basket with empty jars and fresh eggs the hens had graciously provided this morning. Perhaps some of the herbs from her garden and aromatic plants that grew better near the sea could be sold in the tea shop and earn her a bit of coin. She added several bundles to the basket. The traveling merchant always took items on trade, but not everyone in town did.

She cinched the basket's strap around her wrist and stepped into the salt-damp morning. The air was cool and restless, the kind that promised weather later, though not yet. Perhaps late today or early tomorrow. The path bent inland from the lighthouse, a ribbon of earth that disappeared into the trees.

"Going somewhere?"

Evran's voice carried easily over the wind. He was leaning against the fence near the hens' lean-to, coat half-fastened, hair still damp from where he had splashed his face at the pump.

"I need supplies. There's a town about an hour's walk down the path," she said simply.

"I'll walk with you."

She hesitated. She didn't need a companion. She didn't want a witness. But his tone was matter-of-fact, not intrusive, and she found herself nodding. She had no good reason to say no, at least not one she was willing to share.

They set out together, side by side at first, then drifting into an easy rhythm as the trail narrowed and dipped beneath overhanging branches. Salt still clung to the air this far from the lighthouse, softened now by the scent of damp earth and the faint sweetness of last night's rain warming on sunlit leaves. Gravel shifted under their boots in a steady counterpoint to the distant rush of the sea.

Thessa adjusted the basket against her hip, mindful of the early stiffness that hadn't quite loosened. He noticed—she could tell by the quick flick of his eyes toward the way her fingers tightened on the handle. But he didn't mention it. For that, she was grateful.

The silence stretched, but instead of growing sharp, it gentled, like a fog thinning as morning settled in. She let it stay for a while before nudging it open.

"Do you always travel alone?" she asked, shooting him a curious look.

He shifted the worn leather satchel on his shoulder and she noticed him stiffen slightly. "Usually."

"That doesn't sound restful. Wouldn't it be easier with a companion to share the work?"

"It isn't meant to be restful, it's meant to be peaceful." His mouth twitched faintly, like the edge of a smile that never fully formed. "Some things are easier to leave behind when you don't stay anywhere long."

The words were careful, but the space between them was heavy. She heard what he didn't say more than what he did and decided to press further. Maybe she could help just by listening to his story.

"What kinds of things?" she asked gently.

He looked toward the trees, where the wind fretted through the branches, stirring shadows in restless patterns across the path. "Memories. People. Places that no longer fit."

The answer was true, but thin. Like fabric worn by years of use, revealing more in what lay behind it than in the words themselves. She wanted to ask more, but the tension in his jaw warned her off. He wasn't ready to let anyone see past that weave. She let the silence return, filling it with the rustle of leaves and the steady rhythm of their boots on the path.

His grief walked beside him, unspoken but undeniable. She knew its shape. Different from her own, perhaps, but kin all the same.

They walked for several breaths without speaking, each trapped in their own thoughts.

Evran broke the silence. "You know, for someone who claims to live a quiet life, you attract a surprising number of feisty creatures."

"It's more like they find me," Thessa replied letting her gaze drift over until she saw he was watching her and then she focused on the ground in front of her.

"Hmm. Should I be worried I'm next on the list?"

"That depends. Are you feisty?" she asked with a smile.

"Only on special occasions," he answered. When she chanced another look at him she was rewarded with a crooked grin.

She looked away quickly, but this time instead of embarrassment there was a warmth that lingered in her chest.

By the time the trees thinned and the first roofs of the village appeared between the branches, she felt a shift in her own body—her shoulders tightening, her breath shortening against the old memories waiting ahead. She lifted her chin, steeling herself, and tightened her grip on the basket as if its simple weight could anchor her for what came next.

The cobblestones came sooner than she was ready for. One moment there was the hush of the path, trees bowing and sighing around them, and the next there was the hollow clack of her boots striking stone, the faint smell of hearth smoke and baking bread, the hum of voices slipping between narrow streets.

Thessa's steps slowed. She didn't mean them to. Her body recognized the place before her mind could argue. Her shoulders crept upward; her jaw set tight. She lowered her gaze just enough to avoid the stares she already felt pricking along her skin.

A bell over the baker's door chimed as they passed. A woman bent to her daughter, whispering, "That's the keeper, the paper one." The child peeked with wide eyes, then ducked behind her mother's skirts.

She risked a glance over at Evran to see if he had heard but his gaze was focused straight ahead, expression unreadable. She really wished he had let her come alone. She didn't want him seeing this version of her. The one filtered through other people's superstition and pity.

Near the well, an older man gave her a solemn nod, as though she carried some sacred duty he dared not disturb. He grasped a religious talisman hung on a cord around his neck and his lips moved faintly in a blessing.

Further on, two young merchants paused mid-conversation and eyed her with sideways glances.

"Strange, a young woman living alone out there," one muttered, probably thinking he was quiet enough she couldn't hear. "Storms for company and no one else."

His companion snorted. "Well, not alone today. Maybe the keeper's finally tired of playing the hermit."

Thessa gripped her basket tighter, the edge of the handle biting into her palm until her fingers cramped.

She had forgotten how loud the village was. How the noise carried as much weight in the looks as in the words. Reverence. Pity. Suspicion. None of them saw her whole. Not here. It was why she had left.

Evran matched her slowing pace without comment. He walked quietly beside her, but she felt him watching, felt him take in each stare, each muttered word. The faint crease forming between his brows. The subtle tightening of his jaw. He saw more than she wished he would.

His hand brushed gently against hers but when she glanced over in surprise he was still looking straight ahead with just a hint of tightness in his jaw. Had it been an accident or was he trying to reassure her without drawing extra attention to her?

Here, she was never just Thessa. She was the girl whose mother had died too young. The daughter whose father passed before she'd found her footing. The frail one. The odd one. The keeper with magic folded into her fingers but pain folded into her joints. The woman with no husband. No family.

Her throat ached, dry as the paper she meant to buy.

She forced herself to straighten and took a deep breath. The list was simple: paper, oil, flour, ink. That was all. Nothing more. If she kept her mind fixed on the list, perhaps she could finish before the weight of their stares wore through the last of her nerve.

Evran's voice came quietly, meant only for her. "This is where you lived before and why you keep to the cliffs."

She nodded almost imperceptibly but didn't speak. Glad that she didn't need to. It had been more of an observation than a question.

The paper-maker's shop smelled of pulp and ink and damp wood. Sheets hung from lines like pale skins, some rough and fibrous, others fine as breath. Thessa's fingers itched with longing even before she stepped inside.

She had traded eggs for flour. Sold her dried herbs at the tea shop for enough coin to get some oil. The empty jars in her basket were now full and the basket heavier.

She only had this stop, her favorite shop left, then she could return home. She could almost take a full breath.

Evran examined the fancy quill pens in the front window display. Giving her space to look around all she liked.

She wove carefully between stacks of parchment and jars of pigment, the basket steady at her side. As she reached for a tin near the counter, the kind her father had always favored, dark lacquer marked with faint calligraphy, her grip faltered.

The joint in her thumb locked just as she lifted. The tin slipped from her hand, struck the counter's edge, and hit the floor with a sharp crack. The lid came loose and ink fanned across the stone floor in a black, widening bloom.

Gasps. Quick steps.

"Oh, love," the shopkeeper's wife clucked, already hurrying forward with a rag. "Your hand. Don't strain yourself."

Behind her, a faint whisper: "Poor thing, it's gotten worse."

Heat roared up Thessa's neck. Her chest tightened, every breath shallow and sharp. Not here. Not in front of them. Not again.

The stain bled wider across the floor, catching the lantern light. Every eye felt like pressure on her skin, every murmur a needle. She clutched the basket to her ribs, hands trembling, knuckles white.
Her heart stuttered—too fast, too loud.

The room blurred. The sharp scent of ink filled her nose, thick and clinging, until she couldn't draw breath at all.

"I…"Her voice broke. She set the basket on the counter before her hands shook badly enough to drop it. Then she turned sharply and pushed past the threshold into open air.

The chill wind hit her full in the face, but it didn't clear the panic choking her. She hurried around the side of the building and pressed herself against the outer wall, palms flat to the stone, gasping like someone drowning. *Get away, get away, get away.*

But her legs had locked. She couldn't run. Couldn't go forward or back. The world swayed with her ragged breaths, every sound amplified—the rumble of a cart's wheel, the chatter of children, the scrape of boots behind her.

"Thessa."

It was Evran's voice. Low. Smooth. Calm.

He didn't touch her. He only crouched near, his presence solid as the wall at her back. In his hand, her basket sat upright and steady, as if to remind her that something in this moment wasn't falling apart.

She squeezed her eyes shut, fighting for breath. Shame clawed up her throat. *I should leave. I shouldn't have come. I should go back to the sea where no one watches me break.*

But paper and ink were essential to her work. People would suffer without her folds. She was an adult, not a child to be shuttled away when things grew hard. She drew a breath, held it, and let it go slowly.

When she finally spoke, her voice was cracked but steady enough. 'I need… I need to finish.'

Evran inclined his head. No questions. No pity. No offer to take over. Only a quiet acknowledgment that this was something she needed to do and that he would wait.

She pressed her hand to the stone once more, grounding herself. The wall was cool beneath her palm, unyielding. Steady. She drew one breath, then another.

When she opened her eyes, he was watching her. No pity. Only patience, quiet and unwavering, as if he understood without needing her to speak.

She lifted the basket from his hands and forced her feet to move. One step. Then another. Back inside.

The mess was still there. The whispers had faded and the other customers had gone about their shopping.

She lowered herself to the ground, took a clean rag from the bucket beside the shopkeeper's wife, and quietly began to wipe the spill away.

CHAPTER 7

THESSA

The bell above the shop door jingled faintly as she stepped out onto the well-worn boards of the shop's porch, her basket tucked against her hip, the needed paper and ink tucked inside. The air smelled of flour and horse leather. The sun was warm on her face as she lifted it. She drew a long breath, willing her hands to steady, grateful that her tasks here were complete.

On the bench across the way, Evran sat waiting, a brown paper bag balanced casually on one knee. He looked up at her, expression quiet, and lifted it slightly.

"Sandwiches," he said. "Thought you might need one."

Her lips parted with the words she had been ready to speak
— that she wanted to leave, that she couldn't linger in this
place any longer. But before she could, he added:

"I asked about somewhere quiet where we could eat. They
said there's a pond, just outside the village."

The words caught her still. There was a warm certainty in his
voice, an understanding that she would be ready to get out of
town. The kind of understanding she hadn't felt in years —
not since her father's voice had steadied her through storms.
She nodded once, and he rose without question.

"I know the place," she said tipping her head towards the
woods just to the west. She led him down the porch stairs
and started down the path towards the edge of town.

He followed, reaching for her now heavy basket and tucking
the bag of sandwiches inside. "Did you grow up around
here?" he asked walking beside her, keeping hold of the
basket as they walked.

"I did," she answered, "in a cottage just a short walk from the
pond, actually."

"Will you show it to me?" He asked.

"It's not there any longer," she said, grief threading into her
voice before she could stop it. "But I can show you where it
used to be."

Losing the cottage, watching it be demolished, had been its own kind of burial. A quiet goodbye to the place her parents had laughed and loved in. But it had also been a sign that she needed to move forward, to follow a path that was hers alone.

He nodded and continued walking, seeming to sense that she needed a minute to get her emotions back in control.

The path bent away from the cottages, narrowing between birches that whispered in the afternoon light. The sound of the village faded behind them, replaced by the hush of reeds and water.

When the clearing opened, Thessa stopped.

The pond was just as she remembered it — still water cupped by trees, the surface dappled gold where sunlight pressed between branches. A place both ordinary and sacred.

Her breath hitched. Not from pain, but from the sudden ache of seeing it unchanged. The pond was exactly as she'd left it, a piece of her childhood preserved when so much else had been taken.

"This," she said, her voice thin. "This is where I folded my first boat."

Evran didn't speak. He only stood beside her, waiting, his expression betraying just a hint of his own pain.

Her throat worked as she forced the words free. "My father's hands… he guided mine. I was six. We folded for my mother."

"I know places like this," he murmured. "Ones that hold more than you expect."

He nodded to a pair of large stones at the pond's edge as if in invitation to sit and finish her story.

The memory came in fragments: parchment between her fingers, a lopsided crease, the way her father's smile had carried her through. She told it haltingly, piece by piece, until she could see again the paper boat rocking unsteadily on the water before drifting away.

When her words fell silent, the pond seemed to hold them, ripples catching the story as if to carry it forward. Evran's quiet beside her was not empty. It was thoughtful, as if he knew her thoughts were lost in a past time. He simply reached inside the basket and handed her a sandwich.

They sat on the bank, eating their sandwiches. For a long time, neither spoke.

A large dragonfly dipped gracefully among the reeds at the edge of the water, occasionally skimming the pond's surface. Thessa watched it and let her emotions settle, the grief retreating to that place in her heart where it seemed to live permanently. She didn't mind it living there; it meant she hadn't forgotten her parents and the love they had shared with her. It was bittersweet instead of the sharp pain of fresh grief.

Several minutes passed before Evran asked, gently, "What was she like? Your mother?"

Thessa turned towards him and cocked her head slightly. "I remember her laugh, but not her face. I remember the lullabies more than her touch. Most of what I know came from my father — the way he carried her grief, and mine." Her voice wavered and she could feel the tears starting to well up before sliding unbidden down her cheeks. She turned away and lowered her head.

Evran shifted closer. He didn't reach for her right away, only waited until she turned slightly toward him. Then, with careful hesitation, his fingers brushed one of the tears from her skin. His touch was warm, grounding.

Her breath caught in surprise, not just at the touch, but at the gentle expression on his face. The pain she could see behind his eyes that mirrored her own grief.

For a suspended heartbeat, they leaned into the closeness — the air thick with something fragile and unspoken. His hand lingered just enough, his gaze steady on hers. The distance between them narrowed, breath mingling, the world holding still.

Almost.

At the last moment, she drew back just slightly, not in rejection but in uncertainty. The hum between them didn't break, only stretched thin, trembling like a held note.

She turned her eyes back to the pond.

He didn't press.

The silence was full. Not empty.

And the water carried the reflection of their nearness out across the surface, where reeds swayed and time held its breath.

Time passed, how much she wasn't sure, but eventually Evran cleared his throat having moved to the far edge of his stone seat.

"Are you finished?" He asked gesturing to the uneaten portion of her sandwich still resting in her lap. "If so, we should probably get headed back towards the lighthouse, unless you want me to stay in town?" There was uncertainty in his voice, though she could suspected he was trying hard to hide it.

"I am. And if you don't mind coming back for a few more days, I could use some help with the cottage roof. I noticed some of the tiles shifted and broke after that last storm." She tried to sound casual, but the thought of him not being there bothered her for some reason. She wasn't sure why, she had been there alone for years. She chided herself for being so silly, but still looked at him with hope in her eyes.

"I'll stay as long as you need my help," he replied with solid sincerity.

They turned away from the pond when they'd finished eating, following a narrow deer trail that wound through birch and bramble. Thessa's steps slowed as they neared the rise. The air shifted here—quieter somehow, as though the land remembered what once stood upon it.

When they crested the small hill, she stopped.

The clearing was empty. Grass had reclaimed the footprint of the cottage, soft and wild where boards and hearthstones had once rested. A single cornerstone remained half-buried, the only marker of a life long left behind.

Thessa's breath trembled in her chest.

"This was it," she whispered. "My home."

The wind moved through the grasses, bending them in a slow, familiar sway. She stepped forward, her fingers brushing the top of the old corner stone, rough and warm beneath the sun. Memories rose unbidden—her father boiling tea, her mother humming in the doorway, laughter echoing against timbered walls.

The ache was sharp and tender all at once.

Evran came to stand beside her, his gaze not on her, but on the empty space where the cottage had been. His expression softened—not pity, not sorrow for her, but something like recognition.

"I know what it is to come back to a place that remembers you," he said quietly.

The words stole her breath for a moment.

He didn't offer comfort. He didn't reach for her. He simply *stood with her*, holding the silence the way one might hold a fragile thing—careful, respectful, steady.

Thessa let her hand rest on the stone a heartbeat longer before lowering it.

"It feels different every time," she murmured.

Evran nodded.

"It usually does."

They stood together in the quiet clearing, letting the wind speak for the things neither of them was ready to say.

After a while, she turned back toward the path.

"Thank you… for coming here with me."

Evran dipped his head in a small, solemn acknowledgment and followed her back toward the sea.

CHAPTER 8

THESSA

The morning after the village trip came soft and gray, as though the world itself was trying to smooth the edges of yesterday. Thessa rose early, aching more than usual from the walk and the tension it had wrung out of her joints.

She dressed slowly and cleaned her face using the wash basin in her room, though the water she had poured from the pitcher was a bit chilly. She pressed her hands flat on the surface of her bedroom door, grounding herself in the familiar grain of the wood, before heading to the kitchen to begin breakfast preparations.

The kitchen smelled of herbs and bread that had gone slightly stale. Evran was already there, sorting through a pile of cedar shingles he must have pulled in from the shed. His hair was damp and freshly combed. His sleeves were rolled revealing his well-toned forearms and tan skin.

He hadn't shaved in a few days, and she thought the facial hair made him even more attractive. He looked up briefly when she entered and she quickly looked away, slightly embarrassed to have been caught staring.

"Roof looks like it may have more damage than you thought. I think it'll only hold for another few weeks at most and that's if we don't see any more storms," he said, matter-of-fact. "I'll start with the worst of it today."

She nodded, busying herself by filling the kettle and heating the skillet. "I'll be in the garden after seeing to the lighthouse. It needs weeding before the roots take hold. The breeze off the sea seems to make the weeds spread so quickly."

They fell into a rhythm of breakfast—eggs, bread toasted over the coals, tea steaming faintly in mismatched mugs. Their conversation stayed on the practical: shingles, weather, the work each meant to do. Safe topics, held carefully between them. As felt routine now, Evran helped her with the dishes and cleaning up the kitchen.

When the dishes were done, they parted without fuss. He started toward the shed to grab the ladder, and she toward the lighthouse, knowing today was going to be a bit harder with her body already aching.

By mid-morning, the sun had burned through the gray. Thessa knelt among the herb beds, shawl tucked around her shoulders, hands working slowly through stubborn roots. Her back ached, but the steadiness of the task kept her breathing even.

The sharp cry of wings startled her. She looked up just in time to see a sweep of white feathers tipped in purples and blues flash above the fence. The Selara alighted on the garden bench, head tilted, something pale clutched in its beak.

Thessa's breath caught. A message.

The stunning tidebird dropped its offering with deliberate care, a brittle, dried flower, stem bound in twine, and then rose back into the sky, wings scattering flecks of light before vanishing toward the sea. Its visits were always brief, but deliberate. Someone was in pain and needed her help.

From above came Evran's voice. "What in the world was that?" He was standing on the half-mended roof, shading his eyes, staring after the bird as it disappeared over the horizon.

"The Selara," she called back, brushing soil from her palms as she rose. "A message. Someone must be in need of my folding."

He frowned down at her, skepticism apparent in his expression. She sighed but didn't elaborate; his expression bothered her in ways she wasn't ready to think about. She told herself it didn't really matter if he understood; she did, and someone needed her magic enough for the Selara to pay her a visit.

She picked up the dried flower, cradling it carefully as though it might crumble in her hands. She noticed the shaky way the twine had been tied around the stem. Like someone who was just learning to make knots. Probably a child. Most likely laid on a grave as a token of grief and love. Although her hands were aching, she would pour every bit of care she could into what she was about to fold. The grief of a child needed extra tenderness.

In the cottage, she set her inks beside the square of handmade parchment. She paused for a moment to still her own emotions. The grief of a child always stirred her soul and brought back threads of her own grief. Her hands trembled faintly as she dipped the brush, but she worked with care, writing a short line along the lantern's edge: *Your love still reaches them. Let this light reach you.*

When the ink had dried, she dipped her fingers in moonwater and began the folds. Crease, turn, seal. A lantern rose slowly beneath her hands, its walls square and steady. She whispered blessings as she finished her folds, then carried it to the garden where a whistlekin was already waiting.

The little moss-furred creature chirped and bounded across the fence, nearly upsetting the dish of moonwater she had set out.

"Such a troublemaker," Thessa laughed despite herself and held out the dried flower, "Here. This belongs with you."

The whistlekin sniffed, whiskers twitching, then tucked the stem carefully beneath its ribboned tail. When she set the lantern down, it nosed at the folds, chirped once as if in approval, and leapt off the fence—lantern balanced impossibly in its small paws, carried as though weightless.

Thessa watched it bound almost weightlessly across the field and into the forest. As it vanished into the line of trees she marveled at how they somehow always knew how to get her folds to the right place. She supposed it was like how she always seemed to just know what shape to fold and what blessings to say. There was a beautiful balance in their magic.

As she turned away from the trees she noticed movement out of the corner of her eye. Evran was standing near the ladder, quiet, observing. His expression gave little away, but his gaze lingered on the empty sky. His doubt hadn't vanished, but it had softened; his eyes followed the sky with a reluctant wonder he didn't seem ready to name. Faith that simple acts of caring could make a difference didn't come easily.

"I'll start dinner," she said, brushing her hands clean. "Stew should be ready in about an hour."

He nodded, still silent, without moving his gaze from the sky.

The cottage filled with the scent of simmering broth, hearty root vegetables, and herbs by evening. Thessa ladled stew into bowls and set the breadbasket in the middle of the table. She called Evran inside and then poured water into glasses as he washed up at the sink before joining her at the table.

For a while, the talk stayed light: weather, the hens, the way the whistlekin had nearly stolen Evran's bootlace earlier before she had gone outside. When they both laughed, she noticed what a warm, carefree sound his laugh was. The clear sparkle in his eyes when his guard was down was captivating.

86

Then Evran's gaze flicked toward the window, where several of her folds sat on the sill. "That magic you sent out," he said quietly. "Do you really think it helps?"

Her spoon stilled. "I know it does."

He gave a small shrug, not unkind. "I suppose there's no harm in trying. Even if it's just… symbolic."

The word cut sharper than he intended. She set her spoon down, her appetite thinning. "It's more than that. It carries what can't be carried otherwise."

He didn't argue. He only nodded, as though agreeing to disagree.

Thessa's jaw tightened. "You think it's pretend," she said quietly.

Evran blinked. "I didn't say that."

"You didn't have to. You told me before that you think it's symbolic." Her voice thinned with strain. "That's what people say when they don't believe something matters."

"I just meant—" he began.

"That it's harmless, even if it doesn't do anything real," she finished for him, bitterness slipping through. "But it *does* do something real. You saw the Selara today. You saw how it came."

She swallowed hard. "You may not understand it, but please don't diminish it."

Evran's mouth pressed into a line, defensive frustration sparking beneath his calm. "I'm not diminishing it. I'm trying to understand it."

"Are you?" she countered, soft but cutting. "Because it feels more like you're trying to make it small enough to fit into your comfort."

Their gazes held. Hers hurt, his guarded, and the silence that followed was sharp enough to sting.

They ate in silence for a while before he spoke again. "The village yesterday… the way they looked at you." His tone was careful. "They don't know how capable you are."

Her throat tightened. "It's nothing new."

"It shouldn't have to be normal," he said, his frustration in his voice.

"I stopped hoping for better years ago." His words pressed too close, too raw. She deflected, turning the question back on him. "What about you, Evran? What do you carry that makes you keep walking? You never answer."

The shutters came down in his eyes immediately. "It's not a story worth telling."

Did he really expect her to lay her heart bare when he wasn't willing to share even a bit of himself? Her mind flashed back to the conversation by the pond and the almost kiss. That conversation had been all about her too. She pushed back her chair before the tears could rise.

"Then I think we're finished." She gathered bowls, turned her back to him at the sink, letting the clatter of crockery hide the tremor in her hands.

"How much longer will the roof take?" she asked, voice tight.

"Another day, maybe two," he answered after a pause. She swore she could feel his eyes boring into her back.

"Two days. Then it's time for you to move on," she said, somehow managing to keep her voice steady.

The words hung heavily in the room.

Behind her, she heard only the scrape of his chair, then silence. She didn't turn to see his face. She couldn't. Not with a tear carving its way down her cheek.

Moments later she sensed rather than heard him return — the shift of the air, the weight of his presence pressing against the quiet.

"What happened?" His voice was low, almost confused. "I thought something was building between us. Why are you suddenly shutting me out?"

Wiping the tears from her face, Thessa turned towards him.

"Pushing you out?" Her voice trembled, quiet anger sharpening each word. "You've never let me in. I've opened myself to you. My past, my grief, my craft. And in return?"

She shook her head, tears blurring her eyes. "You call my magic symbolic, but what's more symbolic than this; me speaking and you answering with nothing? I've opened my heart to you and gotten silence in return."

Evran stilled, taken aback, his expression unreadable in the half-light. At last, he gave a slow nod, voice low and measured.

"I can't. Just a couple more days. Then I'll move on." He left the room and a moment later she heard the door click shut.

She pressed her damp hands to the counter and let the tears start to flow freely down her cheeks. The silence of the cottage was louder than any storm.

CHAPTER 9

EVRAN

The night air hit harder than he expected. Cool, damp, threaded with salt. It should have steadied him, but instead, it only sharpened the ache in his chest. He leaned against the cottage wall, closed his eyes, and let the silence close around him.

He hadn't meant to wound her. The look in Thessa's eyes, the tear shining in the lantern-light, the fury stretched thin over it. It replayed in his mind until it hollowed him out. He'd only asked, only wanted to understand, but the words had come wrong. They always did when the questions circled too close.

Her voice lingered, sharper than any blade: *You've never let me in.*

He pressed his forehead against the stone. She wasn't wrong. He had given her almost nothing, even while taking in her grief, her past, her magic. Blocking the past with walls kept him moving. Opening those walls was risky. He didn't know if he could.

Memory flickered — smoke, firelight, the weight of a child he couldn't save. He blinked, took a deep breath, and shoved it back before it could take shape.

And yet… the sound of her laugh earlier still lingered. Warm stew. The sight of her folds lined along the sill, fragile but filled with hope. The cottage had started to feel closer to home than anywhere he'd been in at least a decade. That was what terrified him most. Belonging meant the possibility of losing again. Losing was something he wasn't sure he could survive again.

He drew in a slow breath. The only safe choice was the one he'd already made: finish the roof, then leave. A couple of days. He told himself it would be enough.

It had to be.

Above him, the lighthouse beam swept across the water, cutting through fog and dark alike. He tipped his head back, letting its steady pulse wash over him. Comforting, yes, but also a reminder that he was still on the outside of every warm place, watching light meant for other people from the shadows.

The air in the kitchen was heavy when he entered the next morning. A plate of food sat on the table, covered with a towel. He stepped closer and lifted the small piece of paper resting on top:

Headed to the lighthouse early this morning to do seasonal upkeep. Will be busy until dinner, so you can have the leftover stew from yesterday for your lunch.

— T

She was avoiding him. And he had to admit, part of him was relieved to delay the inevitable awkward encounter. She made him feel things, and he'd built an entire life on avoiding his feelings.

The plate she'd left for him felt strangely intimate, a small act of kindness wrapped in distance. She could be furious with him and still think to make sure he ate. The contradiction lodged under his ribs.

He sat and ate the food quickly. The sooner he got started on the roof, the sooner he could be done and move on. Forget about how Thessa's eyes seemed to see straight into the depths of his soul. He wasn't ready to face what was there himself, let alone share it with anyone else.

Evran shook his head and forced his focus back to the task ahead. He'd need to start on the north side of the roof today. It wasn't as battered as the side facing the sea, but it still looked like it had been neglected for years. He was going to hurt her, that felt unavoidable, but he could at least leave her in a better position than before he arrived. He owed her that much for her kindness.

He set his fork down after the last bite, then carried his plate to the small sink and washed it quickly. He refused to be a burden. He steeled himself to finish what needed to be done and move on. Never mind that he had no idea where he would go next—his memories chased him wherever he landed. But as long as he kept moving, maybe he could stay ahead of them.

He set the clean dish on the shelf with the others, drew in a deep breath, and turned to face the day's work. Hard labor was the best way to keep both his mind and his body busy. If he stayed much longer, he was going to care more deeply than he could afford. Maybe he already did. That thought alone unsettled him more than any storm the sea could conjure.

Place a cedar shingle, grab a nail, hammer it in. Repeat. The rhythm of the task was soothing, and his mind needed soothing this morning. He wiped his sleeve across his forehead, catching the sweat before it could drip into his eyes. It was honest work. Hard work. He'd always prided himself on his willingness to face whatever task was set before him. It had served him well since leaving home at sixteen with his best friend Rion to join the sea merchants.

Rion. Well, that was another memory he was doing his best to forget.

After a while he set the hammer aside and eased himself toward the edge of the roof, legs dangling over. From here, he had an unobstructed view of the sea. Sunlight scattered across the surface, turning the water into a sheet of blue glass that stretched on forever.

On days like this, it was hard to believe the sea had taken so much from him—his parents, his sister, so many shipmates, and just two years ago, his best friend. He could blame the sea for all his hardships, but tragedy didn't seem to care whether he was on water or land. It followed him either way.

Just then, something scampered across his legs, and he nearly lost his seat on the edge of the roof. He glanced down to find one of those troublesome little whistlekins perched beside him. It gazed out at the sea with a focus he understood all too well, its mossy green tail swishing lazily back and forth. The creature gave a soft whistle, looked up at him, and nodded once before darting down the side of the cottage.

Evran's eyes followed its path as it approached the lighthouse door and picked something up. When it turned, he saw it held one of Thessa's folded creations—a butterfly. The whistlekin ran forward a few steps and released it into the air. The delicate paper wings caught the wind and drifted out over the water. A moment later the creature scampered toward the garden, nibbling at a few of Thessa's plants before bounding off into the woods.

Evran searched the horizon, but the butterfly was already gone. He had to admit that it felt like more than superstition. Yet if this magic could ease grief, why did his still sit so heavily in his chest? Why did the sight of the butterfly make his breath catch?

It looked so much like the one he'd seen clutched in a little girl's hand a decade ago. The image hit him hard. Small fingers wrapped around the folded shape as she took her last breath in his arms. He swallowed and blinked the memory back into its box.

He stood and returned to the roofline. These thoughts were getting too close to the surface here. He needed to finish this and put as much distance between himself and this place as possible.

He returned to the shingles, but his gaze kept drifting to where the butterfly had vanished. Thessa's magic carried sorrow away with such impossible gentleness.

His own sorrow clung like wet sand, refusing to shift. Some wounds didn't lift with the wind. Some stayed rooted in the bone.

He wasn't sure if even her magic could reach him.

Evran was washing his hands when Thessa walked by and into the cottage that evening. She didn't even look his way. It had been clear that she had been avoiding him all day. But could he really blame her?

He sighed, dried his hands on a towel, and headed for the cottage door. A motion over to his left caught his eye. It seemed like the field had exploded in a flurry of color, vibrant yellow and orange flowers, and some soft pink flowers with heads that seemed to be bursting out of the centers.

Before he could talk himself out of it, he stepped outside and gathered a small handful of the prettiest ones. A peace offering. Or at least… an attempt at one.

Once he was satisfied with the handful of colors he'd gathered, he opened the cottage door and stepped inside. The scent of fragrant herbs and stewing vegetables tangled in his nose. From the kitchen came the soft, steady thump of Thessa's knife.

He swallowed, shifted the flowers in his grip, and stepped into the room.

He cleared his throat and asked, "Do you have a jar or glass I can put these in? I thought they were pretty and would be a nice addition to the table tonight."

Thessa turned. For a heartbeat, as her gaze caught on the flowers, he thought he saw the faintest hint of a smile. Then she smoothed her expression and retrieved a vase from a lower cupboard. She filled it halfway with water and handed it to him.

He reached for it—and promptly fumbled the flowers, nearly dropping the whole bunch against the counter. He caught them just in time, his ears burning.

Thessa's mouth ticked at the corner, so slight he almost doubted he'd seen it.

"I see the field has decided to bloom for us," she said politely. "It was a nice idea to grab some."

"I don't know what they are, but they're pretty," Evran said, easing the flowers into the vase and setting it in the center of the table. "Do you need help with any of that chopping?"

"No, I'm just about done," she replied.

He shifted his weight, then sat down, hoping—maybe foolishly—that she might talk to him again. The thought of the next couple of days being this stiff and quiet made something twist in his chest.

"Are you familiar with any of these flowers?" he asked.

"All of them." This time her smile was real, small but genuine. "I've lived here long enough to know when I have valuable resources growing so close."

She slid the last of the vegetables into the pot and joined him at the table. She touched the small white flowers first.

"This is yarrow. It's good for treating wounds and easing the pain in my joints. I dry it and use it in my tea." Then she touched the purplish flowers with the distinctive raised centers. "This is echinacea, also called coneflower, if you prefer. It's useful for colds."

"And this yellow one here?" he asked, pointing to a cheerful-looking bloom.

"Coreopsis," she said. "It can be used in teas, but I prefer it for adding a pale yellow tint when I make soap."

As she spoke, Evran felt something inside him ease. Shoulders lowering, breath loosening. This was safe ground: work, plants, everyday life. Conversation that asked nothing of him except to listen. He could do that. He *liked* doing that. And the warmth in her voice, even if small, soothed a part of him he hadn't realized had been braced all day.

But then Thessa sighed softly and looked down at her hands, the moment thinning between them.

He cleared his throat and shifted in his seat. The discomfort crept right back in. He fumbled for another safe topic, but she had already risen and crossed to the stove, stirring the pot with quiet focus.

"I'm sorry," he said to her back. "I know it's not fair, but there are some things I'm just not ready to talk about."

"Dinner will be ready shortly," she replied softly before leaving the room. A moment later he heard the muted click of her bedroom door closing.

CHAPTER 10

THESSA

The next morning unfolded much like any other. Thessa and Evran made breakfast and ate together, managing a brittle sort of peace. As long as they kept to safe topics such as the weather, the roof, anything that didn't require vulnerability, they could pretend the tension wasn't there. But by the time the last dish was dried, the silence between them had turned tight and uncomfortable.

Clearing her throat quietly, Thessa looked up into his warm brown eyes. "I'll be gathering more of those flowers you found yesterday to dry," she said, heat rising in her cheeks as she looked away and stepped over to grab a basket. "After that I plan on weeding the garden. If you need anything just let me know." The words tumbled out faster than she intended, propelled by the desperate need to escape those eyes.

It felt like they drew her in. So much warmth, but so much sadness behind them. She sighed, pushing the thoughts of him away before she got lost in the hurt that washed over her every time she thought about him. Every time she wished he would let her in, even just a little.

Outside, she inhaled deeply and turned her face to the sky. The cool sea breeze brushed her skin, and the bright, gentle warmth of the sun wrapped around her aching joints like a balm. Weather like this felt like a small blessing; the sea's damp could be cruel when paired with cold, but today the breeze seemed to lift the heaviness right out of the air.

Her breath hitched a bit as she got closer to the flowers. They really were stunning, like a colorful quilt painted across the field. She noticed a few flowers that Evran hadn't included in his impromptu bouquet. Sunny black-eyed Susans nodded their heads in the breeze. Even some wild bergamot and mint which would be great for her teas. She gathered them into bundles that she would hang from the rafters in the cottage to dry slowly.

After hanging the bundles, she moved on to weeding the garden. It seemed like it was a never-ending task. As she picked small shoots from between the growing herbs, she heard Evran approach the garden gate.

"I, um… ran out of nails. Do you have more somewhere?" Evran asked.

She looked up, squinting into the sunlight catching his face, and stood to meet him at the fence. "There should be some in the storage shed at the lighthouse base. Metal can, blue lid. They might need a quick sanding, the sea air rusts everything. The stone should be on the right-side shelf. Everything going okay?"

"Fine," he said and just stood there a moment looking at her like he wanted to say more. But he just gave her a small nod of his head and turned to head towards the shed.

Thessa couldn't stop the weary sigh that escaped. She liked having him around. She was more caught up on the chores around the property than she had ever been. But it was more than that. She had to admit that in some ways it was a lot less lonely, but in other ways it was harder. It was a different kind of alone when you were sharing your inner thoughts with someone who wouldn't open up in the same way. This kind of alone was almost more painful.

As much as she wished she could just pretend the divide didn't exist, she wished even more that he would care enough to at least try. She could accept that there were parts of himself that he wasn't ready to share, but it felt like he wasn't even going to try to share any part of himself, and she had already had enough of feeling alone even when surrounded by others.

As she stood there lost in thought a sound reached her ears. A soft shriek of sorts and looking up she spotted the Selara gliding across the water at a faster clip than usual. She stepped out of the garden and started walking towards the shore.

The creature landed a few feet away, a dripping scrap of cloth clenched in its beak. It dropped it at her feet, then flicked its head toward the sea before fixing her with an intent, urgent gaze. Thessa nodded, and the Selara launched itself skyward again, wings beating hard as it swept back out over the waves.

Thessa knelt beside the wet piece of cloth. A shiver rushed over her that had little to do with the temperature or the breeze. Usually the Selara only brought small bits of fabric, but this one wasn't, it was bright blue, nearly new except for the seawater soaking it. A small hat. Small enough to belong to a child.

She scanned the horizon, searching for any sign that could explain the Selara's urgency. Nothing. But the Selara never acted without intention.

"Evran!" Thessa called, already striding toward the storage shed, the dripping hat clenched between her fingers.

He looked up from the can of nails, and concern overtook his expression in an instant. "What's that? What's wrong?"

"A child's hat," she said, breath quickening. "The Selara brought it. It's still wet. We may be able to help. Do you see any boats out there?" She scanned the horizon, heart pounding.

"I don't." Evran stepped out into the sunlight beside her. "It's possible they made it to shore already." He kept his voice steady, but she saw the flicker of panic in his eyes.

"Let's search. I'll go light the lantern and then search east, and you start going up the coastline to the west. Do you know how to whistle?" Thessa said, taking a deep breath and knowing that panic never fixes a problem.

Evran nodded and began walking towards the sea. His entire body drawn tight with urgency. She found herself watching him for a heartbeat too long before snapping back into motion. Turning towards the lighthouse she broke into a sprint, her own resolve hardening with each step.

.

CHAPTER 11

THESSA

Thessa had been working her way up the shoreline for only a few minutes when something prickled at the edge of her awareness. She paused, listening hard. The wind hissed across the rocks, waves thundering against the cliff face. Nothing.

She exhaled and kept moving, each step sending a fresh ache through her knees and hips from navigating the unstable terrain.

If she'd thought this through, she probably should have gone west where the ground leveled out sooner. But if there *was* a child out there—soaking wet, terrified, and likely alone. Getting them back to the warm cottage mattered infinitely more than her own discomfort.

A sudden splash cracked through the noise of the surf. Thessa whipped her head toward the sound, heart stuttering.

"Hello?" she called, breath thin.

No answer. Only the relentless retreat and return of the tide.

Her pulse thudded painfully, but she forced her breathing to steady. She wiped her palms on her skirt and climbed onto another line of rocks.

Her foot slipped.

She caught herself with a jolt, bracing a hand against a cold, sea-slick boulder. Pain shot through her wrist, sharp enough to steal her breath. She squeezed her eyes shut for a moment, fighting the tremor in her fingers.

The sea below hissed and tugged, insistent, as if eager to claim whatever faltered.

Later, she bargained with her protesting joints. *You can complain later.* Today someone needed her. She pressed on, trying her best to ignore the pain.

Then, something thin and wavering cut through the roar of the waves.

A whistle.

Barely audible, almost swallowed entirely by wind and surf. She froze, straining to hear it again.

There. Faint, but real.

Evran.

Her heart lurched painfully, and she turned back toward the lighthouse as fast as her aching body would allow.

As she neared the smoother, sandy shoreline, she finally saw him. Evran striding toward her with a figure in his arms. The shape looked too large to be a child, and her pace quickened.

"He has a pulse, but it's faint and he's ice cold. We need to get him warm and dry," Evran called, voice taut even at a distance.

"Is it a child?" she asked, fear twisting inside her.

"No. A man, maybe a few years older than me. I checked another twenty yards up the shore and didn't find anyone else."

Relief and dread tangled inside her. She nodded quickly and veered toward the cottage, determined to arrive first and get the fire blazing. But the unanswered question—*where was the child the hat belonged to?*—gnawed at her like a living thing.

The climb up the hill felt endless. Her legs grew heavy with fatigue, but she refused to stop. She paused only long enough at the woodpile to gather an armload of logs, then pushed the cottage door open with her hip.

A glance behind her showed Evran halfway up the hill. Gratitude swelled in her. Without him, she wasn't sure how she would have gotten the man up here. And searching alone would have cost precious time. Time the man might not have had.

She fed the logs into the embers of the wood stove and coaxed them back to life. Once the flames caught, she set water to boil and began gathering blankets.

The door creaked as Evran entered, carrying the unconscious man. Thessa gestured to the makeshift bedroll she'd prepared on the kitchen floor near the stove, layered with oiled canvas she could peel away once his wet clothing was removed.

Evran knelt beside the man, checking his breathing again, his jaw tight.

Then he stood abruptly. "I'm going back out."

Thessa straightened. "The child—?"

"Yes." His voice was low, strained. "I didn't see anyone, but that doesn't mean he isn't out there. The tide's shifting, and if he's caught on the rocks…" He shook his head. "I won't take the chance."

Thessa took a half-step toward him. "Then let me…"

Evran cut her off, but gently.

"Thessa," he said, voice softening, "your joints won't handle the rocks right now. I barely managed them myself." He hesitated, then added, with real respect, "And he needs you here. If he wakes up disoriented or slips under again… he needs someone who knows what to do."

The words struck her with the truth of them. He wasn't dismissing her. He was trusting her with the more critical role.

She swallowed hard. "Be careful."

He nodded, grabbed the lantern, and disappeared back into the night.

The cottage felt painfully quiet after he left, save for the crackle of the fire. Thessa knelt beside the injured man, wiping seawater and sand from his skin, doing what she could to coax warmth back into his body while listening for any sound outside.

Minutes bled into what felt like hours.

When Evran finally returned, he was soaked, shivering, empty-handed. The defeated look in his eyes told her everything.

"I searched the full stretch," he said, voice hoarse. "There was nothing."

Thessa handed him a mug of tea and wrapped a blanket around his shoulders, grief settling heavily between them.

Late that night, the man began to stir.

Thessa blinked awake, realizing she'd drifted off with her back against the wall. She eased herself to her feet and crossed quietly into the sitting room where Evran slept in a chair, his arms folded loosely across his chest. He looked exhausted. He had gone back out into the dark searching for a child who might never have reached the shore.

"Evran," she whispered, touching his arm lightly. "He's starting to stir."

His eyes opened immediately, sharper than moments before. "Just now?"

"Yes. Not fully awake, but he moved. His eyes opened for a moment."

He pushed himself up from the chair and followed her to the kitchen, sinking to the floor beside the man. Thessa moved to the stove, already setting the kettle and a small pan of broth back onto the heat.

"Would you like some tea?" she asked, knowing warmth would help settle him as much as it would the stranger.

"Yes," he said, voice low but steady now.

Thessa fell into the familiar rhythm of making tea; one she could perform half-asleep after so many years alone at the lighthouse. The soft clink of mugs and the crackle of the stove felt grounding in the tense quiet of the night.

A rough sound behind her snapped her attention back.

The man was awake.

He coughed once, a harsh, scraping noise, and blinked up at them through bleary eyes. Confusion clouded his face, his brows drawing together as if even the dim light hurt.

Evran leaned forward, voice gentle. "You're safe. We found you on the shore near the lighthouse."

The man frowned, struggling to focus. "Did you… find the others?" he rasped, trying to sit up.

Evran placed a steadying hand on his shoulder. "Easy. And no. We looked for hours. There was no one else."

Thessa's heart tightened. Evran had searched the full stretch of shore. If he didn't find the child… the sea may have taken him.

The man sagged back, devastation hollowing his features.

Now that he was awake, Thessa could see he wasn't much older than she was. Maybe in his early thirties. His face lean, stubble only a day old. A fisherman, not a seasoned sailor.

"What's your name and where are you from?" Thessa asked gently.

"My name is Fergus Doyle. I'm from Brannock… village just south of the inlet." His voice cracked. "I was out fishing with my son Finnrick. And my friend Silas. It was only supposed to be a few hours… just enough to get some dinner."

"You don't have to tell us," Evran murmured, but there was something tight in his voice; a flicker of unease, as though the man's grief hit too close to something he didn't want to remember.

Thessa glanced at him, the realization soft and painful. *He fears grief. Fears what it asks of him.*

She herself had long ago understood that sorrow and joy were woven together. Helping people through the edges of grief was part of her calling.

Fergus swallowed hard and continued, the words tumbling now before courage failed him.

"It was just supposed to be me and Silas, but Finnrick… he begged to come. He was so excited. He grabbed his pole and his new fishing hat—" His voice broke, but he pushed on.

"The leak was small at first. Silas reached for the supply box to patch it, but he lost his balance. The boat tipped. He fell, and when he tried to pull himself back in… the whole boat flipped."

Thessa handed him her cooled mug of tea, and he accepted it with trembling hands, letting the warm liquid soothe his throat.

"If I don't say it now," he said, staring at the mug but not drinking, "I don't think I ever will."

Evran's jaw tightened, eyes flickering away.

Fergus continued, voice frayed. "The boat struck Silas when it went over. I tried to reach him, but… he was just gone. And Finnrick…" His breath hitched. "He was clinging to the boat. I held the other side to try to balance it, but the water kept coming in. We were too far out. And then—"

He squeezed his eyes shut, tears spilling freely.

"When I looked back… Finnrick was gone and I swear, although I don't know how…" He stopped a moment and took a deep breath. "I heard Silas tell me to swim for shore and I hoped it meant they were behind me even though I didn't see them."

A single tear slipped down Thessa's cheek. She reached out and rested her hand lightly on the man's arm, offering the only comfort she could. Evran rose quietly and stepped into the sitting room, grief settling around him like a shadow he didn't want anyone to see.

When the man's sobs quieted to trembling breaths, Thessa reached for the small bit of blue fabric the Selara had delivered earlier.

"Is this Finnrick's?" she asked softly.

He stared at it for a moment, face crumpling.

"His hat," he whispered. "Finnrick's hat."

CHAPTER 12

THESSA

The sound of quiet voices met Thessa's ears when she woke the following morning. For a few precious moments, she burrowed deeper beneath her blankets, letting the gentle murmur of Evran and Fergus drift through the walls. The raw edges of yesterday still clung to her skin; it felt as if her emotions had been dragged over coals and left there to smolder.

But she couldn't hide in bed forever.

With a soft sigh she pushed the blankets aside, dressed, and stepped into the kitchen. The voices hushed immediately, and the warm scent of rosemary and thyme drifted from the stove. Evran stood there frying eggs, sleeves rolled up, the early light softening the lines of exhaustion around his eyes.

"Good morning," he said, glancing over his shoulder, his voice gentle.

"Good morning," she replied. She turned to Fergus, who sat carefully at the table, a blanket wrapped around his shoulders like a shawl. "How are you feeling today?"

"Tired," he admitted. "Warm, thanks to you both. But my head… it feels full of fog."

"That's normal," Thessa said, giving his arm a light touch as she passed to prepare tea. "It will take a day or two for your strength to return."

Fergus shifted uneasily. "I thought… perhaps I could try for home this afternoon."

Thessa shook her head softly as she poured hot water over the tea in three mugs and set one in front of him. "Rest today. Please. Shock lingers, and you shouldn't push your limits."

Fergus hesitated, then nodded in gratitude. "Aye. Then I'll stay the day."

Evran began plating the eggs and toast. "We'll take turns with our tasks so neither of us is far," he added. "No one should be alone after what you've been through."

Something warm flickered briefly in Thessa's chest at his words.

He looked steadier this morning, still tired, still carrying a shadow in his eyes, but present. She wondered how he would act today, knowing he was nearly finished with the roof and would be leaving soon.

Their eyes met briefly as he brought the food to the table. She offered him a small, tired smile. It eased something in his shoulders, and he gave a soft exhale as he sat beside them.

After breakfast, Evran and Fergus stepped outside to walk the perimeter of the cottage grounds. Thessa lingered at the doorway for a moment, watching them. Evran set a steady pace, slowing whenever Fergus faltered. He pointed out the sagging section of garden fence, the loose rail that needed tightening, the tools that needed oil before the next storm.

Nothing strenuous. But enough to give Fergus purpose and a bit of distraction from his wounded heart.

Thessa turned toward the lighthouse. The large lantern at the top needed a deep cleaning, but she kept her tasks light today, unwilling to stray too far. She checked the wick, polished a few brass fittings, and left the harder tasks for another morning.

But there was one task she couldn't put off.

She gathered her papers and tools and settled beside the low table by the window, where the afternoon light made the fibers glow. Her fingers hesitated for a breath before she chose a sheet the soft color of dawn. A good color for remembrance. A good color for guiding lost spirits home.

She began to fold.

Each crease required precision and she took her time, letting the movement become a kind of prayer. Not a grand one, just a quiet asking. A wish. A held breath shaped into paper.

"For his wife," she murmured, the words brushing the air like a sigh. "For his boy. For the sea to be gentle if it can't be kind."

The lantern's shape emerged slowly, its corners neat, its seams crisp. She added a thin strip of gold paper along the rim, a small flourish of light. Then she held the finished lantern over her palms, letting its weight settle.

She hoped Fergus would see what she was trying to say without saying it aloud. She couldn't change the sea or bring back those lost to it, but she could give a little light to the darkness pressing in around him.

You're not alone, the lantern said, even if she didn't. Not today. Not here.

Thessa rose carefully and stepped outside to the overlook where the wind tugged at her hair. She whispered a blessing into the lantern's hollow center, sparked the wick with a flick of magic, and released it. The glowing paper drifted upward on the breeze, floating toward the horizon where the water stretched into forever.

She stayed until the pinprick of light vanished, carried somewhere she hoped mattered.

Evran looked up once, catching Thessa's eye from across the lawn. She offered him a small smile. He returned it, warm and soft.

Her stomach fluttered unexpectedly. She could feel the heat on her cheeks blossom and quickly returned to the cottage to busy herself with preparing a light lunch.

By midday, Fergus was visibly tiring. Evran eased him onto a bench in the shade of a willow tree, and Thessa brought out a light brothy soup, herbal tea, and a few soft slices of bread.

"Thank you," Fergus murmured, taking the tea with shaky hands.

"Rest," Thessa said again, settling beside him. "You've done enough for today."

Evran remained standing nearby, wiping dirt from his palms. "If you're willing later, you can keep me company while I mend the broken latch on the woodshed. No hard labor."

Fergus smiled faintly. "I can do that much."

It struck Thessa then how naturally Evran had woven himself into her world. How easily he offered comfort, not with flowery words but with tasks, presence, steadiness.

She felt herself softening toward him in ways that made her nervous. Her heart was more attached than she thought possible after knowing him such a brief time. She was pretty sure it was going to break when he left.

When Fergus finished eating, Thessa turned to him. "If you'd like something to pass the time while you rest, you're welcome to any book on the shelf."

Fergus lowered his gaze. "I… never learned to read," he said quietly, embarrassed.

Thessa opened her mouth to reassure him, but Evran beat her to it.

"Then she can read aloud," he said easily. "If she's willing." He flashed Thessa a half-grin that felt like a tiny sunrise. "I've been told she's got a good voice for stories."

Heat touched her cheeks. "I'll read," she said softly. "After supper."

Fergus's shoulders relaxed. "I'd like that."

Evran's eyes held hers for a heartbeat too long before he turned back toward the toolshed.

The three of them shared a simple supper that evening. Root vegetables and salt-preserved rabbit roasted with herbs, a loaf of bread warmed by the fire, and tea sweetened with a little honey.

When the dishes were done and the hearth glowed low and steady, Thessa carried a battered but beloved copy of *Treasure Island* into the sitting room.

Fergus rested back in the armchair, eyes half lidded. Evran sat on the rug near the fire, one knee bent, slowly mending a tear in the sleeve of Fergus's weather-worn coat.

"Ready?" she asked.

Both men nodded.

And she began to read.

Her voice floated through the room with quiet warmth. The story was one her father used to read to her — a tale of a boy getting mixed up with pirates while searching for buried treasure. The words tasted like nostalgia and salt and safety.

Fergus relaxed visibly, breath evening out.

Evran's stitching slowed. His gaze lifted to her. Soft, intent, unreadable in the firelight.

She felt her cheeks warm and nearly choked on her words. She had to take a calming breath before she continued reading.

Outside, waves whispered against the shore. Inside, the cottage felt full in a way it hadn't in Thessa's years there. Three souls gathered under one roof, healing by proximity, by story, by warmth.

Thessa read until Fergus drifted to sleep and the fire sank low.

When she finally set the book aside and rose to stoke the coals, Evran's voice reached her quietly.

"You made this place feel like a home tonight."

The words caught her off guard, landing somewhere deep beneath her ribs.

She looked at him and felt something inside her shift in soft, dangerous ways.

"Goodnight, Evran," she said, voice unsteady.

"Goodnight, Thessa."

The lighthouse beam swept past the window, steady and sure. And for the first time in a long time, she felt something steady in herself as well.

CHAPTER 13

THESSA

After breakfast the next day, Thessa and Evran walked with Fergus outside as the man prepared to return home.

"I have something for you," Thessa said, handing him a small, wrapped parcel of food for his journey and a folded crane.

He gently touched the paper bird and then raised his eyes to meet hers. She could see the grief in his eyes soften just a bit.

"Your grief is seen," she said. "Be well."

With that, he shook Evran's hand and turned and began to head towards the wood line to begin his journey back home to his changed life.

Thessa saw the tears streaming down his cheeks, and she felt Evran's eyes on her as she wiped her own away.

"The loss of a child is just unimaginable," she said.

His reply was simply a nod.

Taking a deep breath and gathering in her emotions, Thessa asked, "How is the roof coming?"

"Just about done, maybe another day or two and you should be good for years and all the storms ahead," Evran replied quietly.

The expression on his face was hard to read. Was it regret? Sadness? She wasn't sure and knew he probably wouldn't appreciate her asking.

She swallowed, steadying herself. Talk of roofs and storms was easier than talk of departures. "I have a full morning of things in the lighthouse and then I will be foraging in the woods this afternoon. Would you like to join me in foraging?"

"I would like that. I'll make some sandwiches for lunch and then we can head out. It's a good time for gathering berries and maybe even a few mushrooms."

With that they both turned to set about their tasks.

Thessa began walking towards the lighthouse but turned to say something to Evran about the previous night, but then she thought better of it. Maybe it was just best not to push. He would either open up or he wouldn't and she really shouldn't care either way, but she did.

She sighed and went to gather the tools she would need to take apart the large lantern at the top of the lighthouse. It was time to tackle that deep cleaning so that it would always be there to guide lost souls to safety.

Thessa had no more than opened the door to the lighthouse that afternoon when she heard Evran yelling and quite a commotion over by the garden. She looked and couldn't help but clap a hand over her mouth to hold in a laugh. Evran was chasing all four chickens around the yard and every time he got close they would flit away and he would miss.

"Need some help," she called setting down her box of tools and jogging over to lend a hand.

He looked up at her and smiled sheepishly.

"I think I forgot to latch the coop this morning," he admitted with a slight blush coloring his cheeks. Or maybe he was just turning red from the exertion of trying to catch up the girls.

"It happens," she replied trying to keep her amusement out of her tone.

She pointed at a light tan chicken that had stopped up on the top rail of the garden fence.

"That's Winnie, she'll be the easiest to catch. You just need to move very slowly and hum," she did just that, creeping closer and closer to Winnie. When she was close she quickly caught her legs in her hand and gently lifted the rest of her into her arms.

"You made that look way too easy," Evran laughed with appreciation in his eyes. He walked over the open the coop door to allow Thessa to put Winnie away.

"Ha! She just makes it look that way. Wait until we go for Hildie," she said with a smirk.

"So you're saying we should try for Jane or Tillie next," he asked with an answering grin.

"Absolutely," she said, laughing.

"Any tricks for them?" he asked with a hopeful glint in his eyes.

"Nope, but I think if I distract them with a little grain that you could maybe sneak up behind and grab them up."

"Worth a try," Evran said grabbing a little grain and putting it in the feeding bucket before handing it over to Thessa. Their fingers brushed just a bit when he handed the bucket over and she felt a tingle shoot up her arm. This man was too appealing for her own good.

She walked over to the small clearing to the right of the garden where the remaining three chickens were pecking in the dirt for insects. She sprinkled just a few grains of their feed on the ground in front of her while Evran circled around the left side of the garden to come up behind them.

She crouched down and talked to the girls softly, sprinkling a few grains at a time to keep them focused on her hand and the bucket. She saw Evran's movement out of the corner of her eye as he snatched up Tillie with a quick arm around her body. Thessa quickly reached out and grabbed Jane when she turned to see why Tillie was making such a fuss.

They shared a quick look of triumph as they put Tillie and Jane into the coop.

"Now the hard one," Thessa said with determination.

"You are amazing," Evran said shaking his head, "I'd have been chasing them til' dusk at the rate I was going."

Thessa giggled and then stopped. When was the last time she had giggled? Not since before her father had died she realized. She took a deep breath realizing she wouldn't just miss the help Evran had been giving her around the place, but him, his humor, his companionship.

"I wish…" she started but just when she was about to tell him that she wanted him to stay if he would just open up to her a bit, he dashed off around the back of the garden where Hildie had fled when the other two girls were being caught up.

"Thessa, come see," he yelled stopping and staring at the ground behind the garden with a huge grin.

She did just that and as she got to where she could see behind the garden she giggled again. There was Hildie backed up against the fence with two whistlekins advancing on her. It looked like they had herded her for them.

Evran and Thessa looked at each other with shared delight.

"Thanks for the help friends," Thessa told the whistlekins as she grabbed up a very unhappy Hildie. She took the rest of the grain from the feed bucket and dumped it in a small pile in front of the whistlekins as a thank you.

As Evran and Thessa walked the short distance to the coop, she could feel his eyes on her and the warmth emanating off of his body.

"Thessa, I'm sorry I keep so much to myself. There's just a lot I'd like to forget. Seeing Fergus deal with all of that grief, it's really stirred things up," he said softly.

She decided not to press and instead reached over with her free hand and gave his hand a small squeeze.

The late light stretched across the garden, gilding the fence posts and the distant shimmer of the tide. The Whistlekins had drifted away to wherever they went when their task was done, leaving the air oddly still — peaceful, if fragile.

"Come on," she said softly. "Let's get supper started before the wind decides to change again."

Evran smiled faintly and fell into step beside her. Inside, the cottage smelled faintly of salt and rosemary from breakfast, the familiar scents wrapping around her like a well-worn shawl. He stirred the embers in the hearth while she gathered onions and root vegetables, their motions comfortable in their simplicity.

They worked together easily, unspoken rhythm settling between them. He peeled while she chopped; he set the kettle on while she reached for herbs hanging from the rafters. The scrape of the knife, the quiet clink of pottery, the low crackle of fire — it was all so ordinary it nearly made her ache.

When the stew began to bubble, Thessa leaned against the counter, watching him test the broth. "You're getting good at that," she said.

He glanced over his shoulder, one brow lifted. "At cooking?"

"At staying," she said, and immediately wished she could take it back.

But Evran only paused for a heartbeat, then smiled — slower this time, thoughtful. "Maybe I am."

They carried their bowls to the small table by the window. Outside, twilight had begun to gather over the sea, the light turning from gold to violet. The day's tension melted into something quieter, softer.

"This place gets under your skin," he said after a while, spoon idle in his hand. "The rhythm of it. The air. The quiet. I used to think I'd go mad if I stayed anywhere too long, but…" He trailed off, gaze drifting toward the lighthouse. "For the first time, I can almost picture it. Not moving on. Not needing to."

Thessa's heart gave a small, startled flutter. She focused on her bowl, pretending to cool a spoonful of stew.

"You'd tire of it eventually," she said, more to test him than to argue. "The storms. The stillness."

He shook his head. "Maybe not. Maybe this is the kind of place that changes you without you realizing." His eyes lifted to hers then, quiet and sure. "Maybe some of us need that."

Something in her chest tightened, equal parts hope and fear. She smiled, small and uncertain, and looked down before he could see too much in her face.

They finished the meal in companionable silence, the kind that spoke of trust more than distance. When Evran gathered the dishes, she almost told him he didn't need to — but he only smiled and said, "Let me. It feels good to do something ordinary."

As the last of the light faded beyond the window, Thessa sat at the table, her chin resting lightly in her hand. For the first time in weeks, the house felt full instead of echoing. She could almost imagine this — the steady rhythm of shared work, quiet conversation, laughter in small moments.

Almost.

But the thought of his leaving still tugged at the edges of her mind. Maybe, she thought, maybe he just needed time. Maybe staying could become a choice, not a burden.

The warmth lingered long after the dishes were set to dry, but the thought of losing it pressed sharp beneath her ribs.

CHAPTER 14

THESSA

The tide had slipped low again by the time the sun began to sink. Thessa sat in the sand where the waves whispered against her boots, a small, folded boat resting in her palms. She turned it slowly between her fingers, feeling the ridges of each crease — sharp, clean, precise.

Her father had always said a steady fold came from a steady heart, but she'd learned that sometimes it was the folding itself that steadied her. The paper caught the light like thin glass, its edges golden where the sun touched.

For once, her hands didn't ache. The long days working beside Evran; hauling wood, mending, stirring, carrying — had strengthened her in ways she hadn't expected. The ache of loneliness had dulled too, replaced by the rhythm of shared work, shared silence.

She drew a deep breath. The air tasted of salt and warm stone and something faintly sweet like wild thyme from the cliffside. The horizon stretched endlessly before her, vast and shimmering, and for a moment she felt herself small within it, as if she were one quiet thread in a great woven sky.

It was humbling, that smallness — comforting, even. Here, with the sea breathing in and out and the wind teasing loose strands of her hair, she could feel the world continuing, unbothered by grief or memory. She wasn't its keeper. She was simply part of it.

The boat trembled slightly in her hands as the wind shifted, lifting the edge of one delicate fold. She smiled faintly, smoothing it down.

"Not yet," she whispered. "You'll have your journey soon enough."

The sea answered with a hush against the shore.

Behind her, gulls wheeled low over the cliffs. Somewhere up near the cottage, the sound of hammering had long since faded. The roof nearly done, she knew. Tomorrow, perhaps, the quiet would return for good.

She tried to imagine it. The stillness of the lighthouse without his laughter, without the easy rumble of his voice filling the corners. It should have brought peace. Instead, it left an ache just beneath her ribs.

The sun slipped lower, and the first threads of night began to color the water in violet and rose. She watched the horizon, the paper boat balanced lightly in her open palms and breathed as if to memorize the shape of this moment. Her hands, the sea, the fading light, and the gentle reminder of how wide the world could be.

Evran

He spotted her from the path above the dunes. Her small figure standing out against the burnished edge of the sea, the sunset folding itself around her like a secret she hadn't yet told.

For a moment, he thought about turning back. The evening air had cooled, and the half-mended net waiting by the cottage door would give him an excuse to stay busy, to keep from wanting what he shouldn't. He was leaving soon. He'd told himself that enough times it should have settled by now.

But it hadn't.

Something in the way she sat there; still, steady, hands cupped around a folded boat held him in place. He remembered this morning, when Fergus had left with the crane she'd made for him. The man's spirit had seemed drained but after touching the small bird his eyes had filled with something Evran couldn't name. Hope, maybe. Or peace. Whatever it was, it had been *real*.

He drew a slow breath, tasted salt, and before he could think himself out of it, started down the sand. Each step sank soft, like a heartbeat in slow measure.

When he was close enough for his shadow to stretch across the tide line, he cleared his throat gently.

"Mind if I join you?"

Thessa looked over her shoulder, surprise giving way to a small smile. She nodded and shifted, making space beside her.

He sat, leaving a respectful distance, and for a moment neither spoke. The world had gone gold and violet, waves curling like ribbons at their feet.

His gaze drifted to the paper boat in her hands. "Who's it for?"

"I don't know," she said quietly. "Sometimes I fold just because there's always a need for comfort and peace."

He nodded, eyes on the small creases gleaming in the last light. "I used to think what you did was… symbolic. Pretty, but not much more than that."

Her brow lifted slightly, but she didn't speak.

"I was wrong," he said, voice low. "I saw what that crane did for him. Fergus. It wasn't just a gesture. It was like you gave him back a piece of something he thought he'd lost forever."

Her eyes softened, though the corners glimmered with unspilled tears.

"May I?" he asked, holding out his hand.

She hesitated, then placed the folded boat in his palm. The paper was warm from her touch. He stood and walked to the edge of the surf, crouching where the water whispered against the sand.

For a moment, he simply held it there, feeling the pull of the current, the fragile weight of faith in his hand. Then he set it free. The boat rocked once, twice, then began its slow drift out into the dusk.

When he turned back, Thessa was wiping at her cheeks.

"Hey," he murmured, kneeling beside her. "Hey, it's alright."

She shook her head, a watery laugh escaping. "I don't even know why I'm crying."

He smiled softly. "Maybe because it matters."

He reached out then, not bold, just steady. He let his hand brush her arm before settling over her fingers. She didn't pull away. The warmth of her skin, the tremor of shared quiet, settled between them like the tide drawing in.

The paper boat floated farther out, its faint reflection trembling in the dimming light, and they sat there without feeling the need to say more.

❧

Thessa

She leaned toward him before she quite meant to, drawn by warmth and steadiness. The sleeve of his shirt brushed her shoulder, rough with salt and sun, and that small contact undid her.

The tears came without warning. Not sharp like before, just a quiet spill of everything she'd been holding. Anger that had softened into sorrow, the echo of the fisherman's grief, the endless hum of her own loneliness.

Evran didn't speak. He simply wrapped an arm around her, tentative at first, then firmer when she didn't pull away. His hand rested at her back, the slow movement of his thumb tracing calm into her breath.

"I'm here," he murmured. Nothing more. No promises, no explanations. Just that.

She pressed her face against his shoulder, the scent of sea and woodsmoke filling her lungs. For the first time in days, she let herself breathe without bracing for the ache that always followed.

The waves moved in their patient rhythm. Each time they broke, she felt a little more of the weight she carried seep into the sand beneath them.

Her voice, when it came, was hushed. "Everything just feels… too big tonight."

He nodded against her hair. "Then let it be big," he said softly. "You don't have to hold all of it."

That undid her again. His words, so simple and undeservedly kind. She stayed there; eyes closed, feeling the steady rise and fall of his chest until her heartbeat found the same rhythm.

When she finally lifted her head, the last of the sun had gone, and the lantern light from the cottage window flickered against the waves. She drew a shaky breath, somewhere between a laugh and a sigh.

"Thank you," she whispered.

Evran's answer was a quiet hum, low and certain, the kind
that said he understood more than words could reach.

Evran

The chill crept in slowly, carried by the wind that always
followed sunset. Thessa shivered against him, and the sound
of her unsteady breath tugged at his chest.

"We should go in," he said softly.

She nodded, but didn't move.

Evran rose first, brushing the sand from his palms, then
offered her a hand. Her fingers were cool in his, delicate but
certain as they curled around his. When she looked up at him,
the fading light caught her eyes—tired, yes, but filled with a
strength that made him forget every reason he'd told himself
to leave.

Something in him shifted.

Before he could think better of it, he drew her to her feet and
closer, his free hand resting lightly at her arm. She didn't

flinch, only looked at him with that same steady tenderness that had been undoing him piece by piece for days.

"You're cold," he murmured, his thumbs tracing slow lines along her sleeves. Her skin was softer than he'd imagined, warmth gathering under his touch.

She drew a shaky breath. Half a sigh, half something else. The sound of it stole the air from around them.

For a heartbeat, they simply stood there, eyes locked, the world narrowing to the quiet between them and the rhythm of the sea. Then she took a small step forward.

Evran's pulse stuttered. He let instinct override hesitation, sliding his hands up her arms until they framed her shoulders. He could feel the faint tremor of her breath as he bent his head, his thumb grazing the curve of her bottom lip. Her cheeks flushed at the touch, but she didn't look away.

He didn't know who moved first, only that the distance vanished.

Her lips met his softly, tasting of salt and warmth and the lingering sweetness of her tea. He gathered her in, hands sliding to her back, feeling the fragile certainty of her leaning fully into him. The kiss was gentle, unhurried—an offering, not a demand.

When they finally broke apart, she stayed close, her forehead resting against his. The night hummed around them, insects chirping in the tall seagrass.

Evran exhaled, still tracing small circles at her back. "Thessa…" he began, but the words faltered.

She only smiled faintly, eyes closed. "You don't have to say anything."

He didn't. He just held her there, letting the quiet speak for them both.

Above them, the stars began to appear. One by one, as if the world itself were unfolding.

CHAPTER 15

THESSA

She woke to sunlight already climbing the far wall, a warm ladder of gold she almost never saw from her bed. For a breath, she lay still, suspended between the cotton-soft quiet of morning and the faint, familiar ache that threaded her hands and knees. Late, her body told her. Later than she allowed herself.

She could hear the faint sound of waves crashing in the distance and the occasional breeze rattling the glass panes in her bedroom window.

Thessa pushed herself upright with care, palms flat to the quilt, then the bedpost, letting joints wake in their own reluctant order. The air smelled faintly of cinnamon and grain. Her stomach answered before her thoughts did.

In the kitchen, the stove kept a thin breath of heat beneath a covered pot. When she lifted the lid, steam curled toward her face: porridge, thick and creamy, the surface stirred just before it set. Beside it sat a wedge of last night's bread, sliced and toasted, and a small dish of honey she usually saved for storms.

A scrap of paper waited under the spoon.

Roof before noon. Eat first.

—E

The note was practical, as plain as the bowl and spoon, but the steadiness of it loosened something she hadn't realized she'd cinched tight. She traced the E with her thumb. The letter wasn't ornate, only sure. He had thought of her— quietly, without ceremony, the way roofs were repaired and shutters latched.

She carried the bowl to the table and sat. The first bite was comfort more than taste, heat easing the stiffness in her jaw, the sweetness turning the edge of morning into something gentler. She ate slowly. Her hands remembered how to hold a spoon without rushing.

And then memory threaded in, soft as tide pulling around the ankles: the lantern room's hush, the steady breath of flame, the ache of wind beyond the glass. His hand. Warm, callused, closing around the base of the lamp when she asked. The way he didn't crowd her steps, only steadied what needed steadying.

Other moments followed, rising unbidden.

The quiet picnic by the lake after their trip to town, sunlight resting on the water and the surprising ease between them. The way he moved through her kitchen without asking, finding bread, finding herbs, finding a rhythm beside her as if he had always known where he belonged. How he found things to fix that she hadn't even noticed needed fixing.

Small things. Ordinary things. But together they had shaped something steady, something warm.

And last night had simply been the moment when all those threads pulled tight.

His mouth had been warm and uncertain, the kind of first kiss that asked a question rather than answered one. He tasted of tea and salt. He'd exhaled, quiet and surprised, the second their lips met, like the sound a man makes when he sets down a weight he didn't know he'd been carrying. She had answered with her own intake of breath, the soft catch of a door opening inward.

They had parted on the gentlest edge—foreheads resting together for a single heartbeat. No rush. No claim. Just yes, a small one, but real.

Thessa set the spoon down and wrapped her hands around the warm bowl. The cottage looked different for having held that moment. The window light felt brighter on the grain of the table. The kettle seemed to belong more firmly to its hook. This, her mind whispered, is what it could be like. Not a blazing dawn. A steady warm.

She had never dared dream of sharing her life with a man. In town, when people looked at her and saw only the ache in her hands and the oddness of her craft, love had seemed like a story meant for other lives. Here, where solitude fit like a well-mended coat, companionship had been something fleeting or viewed from a distance.

But now the thought rose of its own accord, new and dangerous and bright. A second bowl on the table. His laugh in this room when the whistlekin stole a crust. Shared work, not because she could not do it, but because the doing together changed the task's shape. She could see, only for an instant, small fingers learning careful creases, a child's brow furrowed in concentration as paper shifted into boat or moth or lantern in a pair of hands steadier than hers would be by then. She could hear the uneven rhythm of small feet on these boards and feel the shake of the railing when someone too short for it tried to peer out at the sea.

Her chest tightened. Not with pain. With the ache of wanting.

She did not pretend she didn't fear it. Wanting made edges sharper. Love was not a charm against loss; she knew that better than most. Her body would not grant her every day she asked of it. There would be mornings like this one, when rising cost careful breath. There would be others, worse. She had built a life measured to her pace. Letting someone inside it would mean letting him see the places where the pace faltered.

She ate a few more bites, then sopped the last of the porridge with the toast and sat back, palms flat to the table to feel the wood. The quiet rang in a different key. She folded the note once and tucked it into the pocket of her dress.

At the sink she rinsed her bowl and set it to dry. Water beaded on her fingers, slid down the faint ink stains at the sides of her nails.

"Careful," she murmured to herself as she wiped the counter. "Not careless."

Hope could turn reckless if held too tightly. She had learned to hold delicate things in her palms, not her fists.

She tied her hair back again, retwisting the braid that always loosened at the nape when she slept. The cottage door stood in its usual square of light, weathered and familiar. She pressed her fingertips to the frame the way she always did and let the cool of the wood steady her.

Outside, the day had the fresh-washed look that comes after a rain. The grass along the path wore a thousand small diamonds of clinging spray. Farther up, the lighthouse threw a late morning gleam across its own glass, the lens bright as an eye in full sun. Near the cottage, a ladder leaned against the eaves. A reminder that the roof was closer to done than she might like.

Evran was already on the roof, jacket folded over the fence rail, shirt sleeves rolled. He moved with that same sure economy, hands and weight making quiet agreements with the wood. He didn't see her at first. She watched for a moment, allowing herself the small, private luxury of it.

The whistlekin announced her anyway, popping up from the rosemary with a scandalized trill that could have meant anything from you're late to he took the good ladder. Thessa huffed, startled into a laugh, and the sound carried up.

Evran glanced down, shade of a smile in his eyes even at that distance. He lifted a hand in greeting; not a wave, exactly, just a small open palm that said I see you.

"I overslept," she called, because saying it aloud made it less like a failing and more like a fact.

"Good," he said, the word dropping warm into the air between them. "Then you needed it."

He turned back to the shingle he'd been coaxing into place. She could have said a dozen other things: thank you for the porridge, for the note, for the patience in your hands, but the words felt large and fragile just now. They could wait.

"I'll check the lantern room," she said instead, "and then I'm in the garden. The thyme means to take the whole bed if I let it."

"Shout if you need a second pair of hands," he answered without looking down, as if the offer were as ordinary as passing a tool.

She stood a moment longer, letting the wind lift the fine hairs at her temple, letting the simple peace of the morning steady her. Then she turned back inside to fetch her basket and gloves.

In the garden, she knelt with a grunt she did not try to hide and pressed the trowel into the earth. The soil gave slowly, then more. The thyme came up stubborn and fragrant. She shook the dirt from the roots and laid it aside to dry for bundles. Work steadied thoughts the way prayer did for other people. The whistlekin supervised from the fence post, pretending not to be eyeing the basket.

"I never thought—" She stopped, not sure who she addressed. The sea, perhaps. The woman she had been, who believed certain doors had closed and locked behind her. Or the man on the roof, who could not hear the rest of the sentence and maybe should not yet.

When she rose at last, brushing soil from her palms, the light had shifted a little, the day edging toward noon. She shaded her eyes to look up. Evran descended the ladder with a bucket of tools bumping softly against his knee.

When his feet touched earth, he looked over at her and smiled. "All done."

The roof was done. His promise to leave sat somewhere between them, quiet and patient, waiting to be spoken aloud.

She wished she knew whether last night had rewritten it… or simply made the leaving hurt more.

The air changed first.

A hush, subtle and heavy, pressed down across the cliffs until even the whistlekin went still. Thessa straightened from the herb bed, hand braced on her knee, and looked toward the horizon. The sea had lost its glimmer, dulled now to slate beneath a gathering wall of cloud. It wasn't the color that unsettled her—it was the feeling. The quiet before a truth arrived.

Wind tugged at her braid, carrying the taste of rain and something electric. She wiped her palms on her apron and looked up at the lighthouse. Its glass caught the dimming light and reflected it back like an unblinking eye.

Evran's hammer paused on the storage shed where he was securing a few loose boards. She could sense him looking out over the sea as she was.
He started towards her; his movements were quick, but sure. By the time he reached her, the first low rumble shivered through the sky.

"Storm's rolling in faster than I thought," he said. His voice carried a new edge. Steady, but alert. "You should head up to the tower. Get the lantern ready. I'll take care of things down here."

"I can help…" she started, instinctively.

He shook his head, already gathering the loose tools into a crate. "You'll help best where the light lives. Go on."

She hesitated, torn between habit and something deeper; the pull to stay, to keep working beside him. But another roll of thunder answered for her, closer now, the kind that vibrated through the chest before the ear.

"Evran…" she began.

He looked up, and for a heartbeat, the wind caught between them like breath. His hair had come loose from its tie, strands whipping across his temple. Rain threatened in the air, sharp as metal on the tongue.

"I'll be right behind you," he promised.

That was enough.

Thessa turned toward the lighthouse path, skirts snapping against her legs. Each step brought her nearer the looming column of stone, its familiar weight both a comfort and a warning. The sky had gone strange—half green, half violet, a bruise blooming across the horizon. She could smell rain now, thick and inevitable.

By the time she reached the door, the wind was a living thing, rushing through the grass and the cracks in the rock. She glanced back once.

Evran moved through the storm's edge like he belonged to it. Tying down the shutter hooks, checking the latches on the chicken coop, his shirt clinging to the lines of his shoulders. A flash of lightning etched him in silver for half a breath before the darkness swallowed him again.

The air thrummed against her skin. The sea heaved, restless and rising.

Thessa pressed a palm to the lighthouse door, whispering the old keeper's prayer under her breath. Not for safety exactly. For steadiness. For light that holds.

She stepped inside and pulled the door shut against the wind.

Outside, the storm gathered its voice.

Inside, her heart answered.

The storm found its way into the lighthouse—not through the stone or glass, but through the silence that settled after. Thessa tended the lantern as if steadiness were a prayer she could keep lit by hand. The brass wheel was cold beneath her fingers, the flame small but certain. Wind groaned against the tower's ribs, and the air tasted faintly of salt and metal.

Evran was a quiet presence behind her. He had traded his soaked shirt for a blanket, though his hair was still damp, curling near his temples. The way he moved was different now, methodical, stripped of his usual easy grace. She could feel the weight of something unspoken between them, heavy as the storm itself.

When thunder rolled close enough to rattle the shutters, he flinched. It was a small movement. Barely a tightening of his shoulders. But Thessa saw it. She turned from the lantern, her voice soft so as not to startle him.

"Evran?"

He didn't answer at first. His eyes were on the sea through the narrow slit of window, the glass streaked with rain and light. "There was a fire in my village," he said finally. His voice was low, distant, as if speaking across years. "Sparked by lightning. I thought I could help. I tried."

Thessa stilled, hands folded loosely in front of her. She knew better than to fill the space with questions. The truth came only as far as it was ready to.

He went on, barely above a whisper. "I carried her out, but… the smoke—" His jaw flexed. "The rest didn't make it."

Silence pressed in, thicker than the air before rain. She could hear the sea hammering the cliffs, the tick of the lantern's wick.

"I'm sorry," she said quietly. It was the only thing that wasn't empty.

He shook his head, a rough exhale escaping him. "Don't be. It was a long time ago. But sometimes…" He glanced toward the flicker of flame. "Storms bring the memories back. The crack, the roar. I can smell it again if I don't keep busy."

Thessa's throat tightened. She wanted to step closer, but held herself still, sensing that any sudden kindness might undo him. "You don't have to keep it out," she said. "You can let it pass through. Sometimes that's the only way the air clears."

That drew his gaze. For a heartbeat, the look between them was too open, too honest. Then he nodded once, slow, and turned back toward the window.

They stood like that for a while; two quiet figures bracketed by storm light. When the thunder began to fade, Thessa moved to the small table and poured the last of the hot tea from the kettle. She held a cup out toward him.

"For the smell," she said gently. "Rosemary and mint."

He accepted it, their fingers brushing for a second too long. "You think of everything."

She smiled faintly. "I try to bring comfort where I can."

The storm eased by degrees, its fury spent. The lantern flame steadied, bright and unwavering. Evran sat on the bench near the window, staring into the dark, and Thessa returned to her work—pretending not to notice that his hands no longer trembled.

For the first time since the waves had carried him to her shore, she felt they were beginning to speak the same quiet language. The kind built from things that didn't need to be said.

CHAPTER 16

EVRAN

She lingered as if she wanted to say more, then only nodded and returned to her work. Evran stood there a moment longer, staring up at the roof, the weight of years shifting—slightly, almost imperceptibly—off his chest.

The morning air smelled of cedar and salt, cool enough to sting the back of Evran's throat as he crossed the yard. The roof was finished, truly finished. He should be packing his things, tightening the straps on his pack, and figuring out where, exactly, a man like him went next.

Instead, he stood in the middle of Thessa's garden staring fixedly at a wooden trellis that had absolutely nothing wrong with it.

Well… almost nothing.

One slat leaned just a bit to the left. Barely noticeable. But once he'd spotted it, his hands were already reaching for the hammer he'd set down after the roofing was done. He gave the trellis an experimental wiggle. It gave just a bit but would hold just fine. No real need for repair.

He set his jaw and fixed it anyway. He might as well since he was still here. It didn't feel right to leave it for Thessa to deal with down the road.

The tap of the hammer echoed lightly in the stillness. It sounded like purpose. Thin, flimsy purpose, but he clung to it all the same.

"That trellis offended you?" Thessa's voice drifted over his shoulder.

He startled, nearly dropping the nail he absolutely didn't need.

She stood a few paces away, her hair swept back by the breeze, her expression unreadable in that gentle way she had. The way the sun made her hair seem to glow from within was lovely, she was lovely. Inside and out.

"It was leaning," he muttered.

"A fraction of a fraction," she said, but there was no judgment in her tone just a hint of humor. Then, more seriously, "I appreciate all you've done. I'm not sure how I would have tackled that roof."

"Glad I could help, but I feel like you'd have found a way to get it done," he replied with sincerity.

She lingered a heartbeat longer as if she wanted to say more. "I'm heating tea if you'd like some."

He nodded but didn't move until she had gone. Only then did he let out the breath he'd been holding. She was… easy to be around. And somehow far more dangerous for it.

Yesterday he'd told her about the little girl he'd carried out of the burning house, the one who had clung to life just long enough to leave a mark he still carried. Saying the words had been like peeling something raw open, yet afterward, he'd felt…lighter. No, not lighter. Just less trapped by the memory.

He pressed the heel of his hand to his brow. Foolish. Dangerous. Opening doors led to places he always regretted. He fixed things. He did not get fixed.

And yet…

He forced the thought away and decided he couldn't face her again right now. So he looked around for something else to repair. The back hinge of the lighthouse door squeaked faintly if pushed at just the right angle. He pushed it. It squeaked. Barely.

Good enough.

He set to work adjusting it until the hinge swung in silence. Then he tightened a stone along the garden path. Then he re-leveled a bucket by the shed. Every job smaller and more pointless than the last.

By midday, even he couldn't pretend any of it mattered.

The sea called to him. Not with comfort, but with the sharp pull of an old wound. He told himself he was only going to fish, only trying to bring something back for Thessa's table. Beneath that practical lie was a raw need to face the place where he'd failed.

The boat creaked as he pushed off, its wood scarred from years of being battered by the sea. The oars dipped in and out with a steady rhythm that contrasted with the unease in his mind.

Then the fog began to roll in, soft and pale, swallowing the horizon. His heartbeat quickened. The air thickened with the scent of salt and memory — and smoke. He hadn't been there when fire took the small ship, but his brain knew the smell too well.

He could see it in his mind's eye, the fire leaping from the deck, his friend Rion's silhouette framed against the blaze, the scream cut short by the boat breaking apart and the sea claiming his best friend. Evran had been safe on shore that day, nursing an injured arm, promising he'd join the next voyage. He hadn't realized there wouldn't be one.

He gripped the oar until his knuckles whitened. "You should've been there," he muttered. "You should've gone."

The fog pressed close, swallowing sky and horizon alike. The world narrowed to the rocking of the boat and the pulse thudding behind his teeth. Lost in his thoughts, he had no idea how far he had traveled from shore.

The fog deepened until the world narrowed to the length of the boat.

Evran squinted, trying to pick out the line where water met air, but everything had dissolved into the same dull gray. His breath hitched. The oars scraped unevenly, the rhythm broken.

"Steady," he muttered to himself, as if his heart ever followed his words.

He rowed harder. The boat drifted sideways. A cold tide slapped the hull, sharper than it should have been, and panic flickered through his chest.

He turned. Nothing but mist in all directions.

Shoreless. Boundless. Breathless.

"Damn it—" His hands trembled around the oars. He tried to align himself by memory, by instinct, but grief had turned everything inside him upside down. His pulse thudded too fast, too loud. His vision blurred. "Not now. Not like this."

A soft flutter broke through the stillness.

Evran froze.

The Selara dropped out of the fog like a falling scrap of starlight, wings trembling as it landed on the bow. Its tiny claws clung to the wood; its head tilted toward him with a strange, knowing urgency.

"What are you doing here?" Evran whispered, voice cracking.

The Selara chirped softly and pressed its tiny beak against his sleeve. A nudge, a plea.

Evran swallowed and reached into the pocket of his coat for the knife he always carried. He cut a button off his coat and hoped Thessa recognized it as his.

He'd pretended not to believe in it. But he was no longer pretending.

He placed the button gently into the Selara's curved talons.

"Take it to her," he said. "Tell her I'm trying to find my way home."

The creature hesitated for only a moment and then launched upward, wings slicing through the fog, disappearing into the emptiness.

Evran gripped the oars again and began rowing in the direction the Selara had gone. "Come on," he whispered. "If she lights the lanterns, I will find the shore. Just hold on."

But the fog thickened still. His chest tightened. For the first time since Rion's death, Evran felt the sharp, icy truth of it: He might follow his friend into the sea.

His breath rasped. The world spun. A wave slapped the hull so hard he lurched sideways, catching himself by the railing. His fingers slipped. The oar knocked loose, clattering against the boat.

"Please," he rasped — he wasn't sure to whom. The sea. Himself. Thessa.

"Not like this…I'm not done yet."

The fog pulsed and the water around him stilled.

And then, like a thread pulled taut from the deep, the air around him shimmered.

Light began to weave itself together on the surface of the water, soft and silver and impossible. It gathered shape, weaving itself into a figure whose edges rippled like a tide.

Every sailor had heard tales of Lirindra. Was it possible she wasn't a myth either? Real like Thessa's magic?

Evran froze, half-kneeling, breath stuck somewhere between fear and longing.

"What do you want of me?" he said, voice thin.

Her reply came as warmth across cold water. Not sound, but memory.
You carry ash that was never yours to bear.

He clenched the oar. "I left him. I wasn't there."

The light pulsed gently and the creature moved close enough that he could see her large eye gazing up at him. *He would not have you join him in the dark.*

Then somehow he heard Rion's voice in his mind. *Life is for the living, Evran. It hurts to watch you forget that.*

His throat tightened painfully. He bowed his head as something in him, something long-tangled, long-festering, cracked.

"I'm sorry," he whispered, voice breaking. "Rion. I'm so sorry."

He let himself cry then, not with the scalding shame of before, but with something that felt like release. The sea rocked the boat gently, as if holding vigil. Threads of light shimmered across the water and the large eye blinked once as a feeling of peace came over Evran. Lirindra closed her eye and sank into the depths of the water.

Silence followed. Not empty. Just…still.

For a long while, Evran simply sat there, letting the sea rock the boat. His face was wet with tears, but they no longer scalded.

A sudden tug at the fishing line startled him. He pulled the rope hand-over-hand until a flash of silver broke the surface — a small fish, gleaming faintly even in the fog.

It felt like a blessing. Or maybe a promise.

"All right," he murmured. "Enough."

Taking the oars in hand, he looked up and saw a thin beam of light break through the fog. He began to row towards it, toward Thessa, toward life, toward the first fragile peace he'd allowed himself to believe in.

CHAPTER 17

EVRAN

The fog clung to the water like breath that refused to leave the body. Evran rowed through it, every muscle trembling from effort and exhaustion.

Life is for the living.

The words pulsed with each oar stroke, threading through the burn in his arms, the sting in his palms, the hollow ache where grief had lived too long.

The sea was so still it felt suspended, as if the world itself had paused to see whether he would keep moving.

Evran focused on the faint glow that flickered through the mist: the lighthouse lantern. His anchor in the fog. For a moment, he thought it might vanish — the way fire sometimes did when the wind took it. He rowed harder. The light shimmered, wavered, then steadied.

"Almost there," he rasped. His voice sounded unfamiliar, scraped raw from tears and cold.

By the time the boat scraped against the pebbled shore, he could barely hold the oars. His whole body shivered with exhaustion, every step dragged up the landing heavy as sodden rope. He barely registered the weight of the small line of fish in his hand. The air near the cliffs was damp and cold, his breath a ghost in the gray.

A shape moved through the fog, a lantern held high.

"Evran! That fog rolled in out of nowhere and you've been gone for hours." Thessa's voice cracked through the mist. Relief, worry, and something softer curling around the syllables.

He tried to answer. Only a hoarse sound came.

When he reached her, she didn't demand an explanation. She simply took the fish from his limp fingers and set them aside as if the small catch were precious.

"You're freezing," she murmured. "Come inside."

He followed her up the slope towards the cottage without argument.

Warmth wrapped around him the moment they stepped into the cottage. The air held the quiet scent of tea and salt and there was a fire burning in the hearth. Evran stood, wet boots dripping on the wooden floor, hands trembling, unsure where to put anything or what to say.

Thessa pressed a warm blanket into his hands. "Sit, get those wet boots off and don't worry about the floor. It'll dry," she told him gently.

He did as she instructed and sat in the wooden chair closest to the fireplace in the sitting room and began removing his boots.

"I'll get them, you get wrapped up in that blanket. You're still shivering," Thessa said, lowering herself to the ground carefully and beginning to help remove the wet boots.

For a long moment he simply watched her work and breathed, trying to steady the storm inside him.

"I saw her," he whispered. "Lirindra."

Thessa froze, breath held. "You did?"

He nodded. "She spoke to me and then brought me a message." The words broke apart, fragile things that barely made it past his lips. "From Rion."

Her expression was curious, but she didn't interrupt.

"He doesn't blame me. He wants me to live." His breath came unevenly.

The words hit like a blow. He curled forward, elbows braced on his knees, hands covering his face.

"But how…" His voice fractured. "How do you live knowing you weren't there? Knowing you…"
He couldn't say it. Couldn't finish the sentence that had caged him for years.

He buried his face in his hands. The sobs came unbidden, sharp and quiet at first, then shaking through him until speech was impossible.

Thessa didn't try to stop him. She knelt beside the chair and rested a hand lightly on his arm. Her voice was a thread of calm through the storm.

"Guilt isn't a debt," she murmured. "It's just grief that hasn't found a place to rest."

She reached for his sleeve, barely brushing it, grounding him with the smallest touch.

"You asked how you live with it," she continued, voice steady in a way hers rarely was. "You live with it the way anyone does… by waking up again tomorrow."

A long breath. Soft. True.

"And by letting someone sit with you when it's too heavy."

He sobbed harder. No longer the sharp, choking tears of guilt, but something deeper, something being pulled loose at the root. The grief didn't scald this time. It emptied. The tide taking what it must.

When the storm inside him finally ebbed, he sagged back, hollowed out, exhausted, but… lighter.

Like the fog inside him had finally begun to thin.

Night settled around them in soft layers of gold and shadow. Thessa had prepared the fish he had caught with wild herbs and fresh vegetables from the garden. After the dishes were done they had gone to the sitting room because Thessa wanted him near the fire.

Now she was resting on the small sofa, her breathing steady, the book she had been reading still open on her lap.

It was past time to head off to bed, but Evran couldn't sleep.

He sat in the chair by the window, watching fog thin against the darkness. The lantern on the table burned low, its flame small but unwavering.

After a moment, he rose and tended to it. Trimmed the wick. Adjusted the flame. Small motions. Steady motions. Motions that made him feel anchored to the world again.

Outside, the faintest hint of stars appeared above the sea, blurred but bright.

"Thank you, Rion," he whispered, letting the words drift out into the night.

For the first time in years, Evran felt like he was breathing clean air. The ache remained, but it had shifted. No longer a gaping wound, but a scar. Something healed enough to be touched.

He turned back to Thessa. The low lanternlight cast her in warm gold, the rest of the room in soft shadow.

"Maybe life is a kind of light," he murmured, barely audible. "Something we tend for one another."

He sat down beside her, not touching, but close enough to feel the steady warmth radiating from her presence.

A quiet promise of what could be began to glow in his heart.

CHAPTER 18

THESSA

Morning broke clear for the first time in weeks. Pale gold light spilled across the sea, turning the water into a sheet of beaten metal. Thessa stood in the lighthouse doorway, hands wrapped around a warm mug as sunlight pooled across the worn floorboards at her feet.

Her body felt stiff and sore, and she wasn't sure if it was from the dampness in the air or because she had spent a good part of the night sleeping on the sofa because she hadn't wanted to leave Evran alone. She supposed it didn't really make a difference; she was going to persist regardless.

The quiet hum of the lantern above felt different today, softer somehow. It wasn't the sound of duty anymore. It was the sound of life continuing. She liked that sound. It was comforting to know that yesterday her work had helped Evran find his way home.

She hadn't even known he was gone until the Selara had brought her his button. Something about the way it had held its body had spurred her into action. The Selara wasn't one to linger. It was then that she had left the garden and looked to see the fog rolling across the sea and the little rowboat missing.

Behind her, Evran was already outside, sleeves rolled, working where the storm had torn the fence loose. She could hear the steady rhythm of his hammer, each strike a heartbeat against the silence. He moved with purpose. No longer a man trying to outrun ghosts, but as one rebuilding his place among the living.

Thessa called, "You'll run out of nails at that pace."

Evran glanced back, sunlight catching in his hair and a small smile forming on his lips. "Then I'll find another way to keep it standing."

"You sound like someone learning to stay," she said before she could stop herself.

Evran stilled, not startled exactly, but taken off guard in a way that softened the lines of his face. He didn't answer. He didn't need to. The truth of it lingered between them, warm as the rising sun.

Later, when the fence stood straight again, they sat together by the small worktable. Sunlight spilled through the window, glinting off the scattered paper scraps that covered the surface. Fragments of Thessa's folded charms, failed creases, and half-finished boats.

Evran reached for one of the paper lanterns she had been repairing, fingertips brushing the faint crease of its edge. "You still make them, even on days like today when it hurts," he said with a hint of wonder in his voice.

Thessa nodded. "Because they help."

He turned the lantern in his hands. "What do they do, really?" There was no judgment in his voice today.

She ran her thumb along the lantern's seam. "They remind the world it's still capable of light." A faint smile touched her lips. "And sometimes they remind me, too."

He studied her for a long moment. She decided she liked the way he looked at her, as if he wanted to know her. She also thought there was a touch of heat in that gaze and that made her heart beat a little faster.

"Then maybe I should learn."

A small ache bloomed behind her ribs. She hadn't realized how much she needed to hear those words. Not because her magic required validation, but because it meant he wanted to understand her world instead of stepping around it.

She wanted to ask him to stay but instead she slid a sheet of spare paper toward him. "Then fold with me."

They worked in companionable silence. The rustle and creak of paper mingled with the distant sigh of waves against the rocks. Evran's first lantern was clumsy, the folds uneven, the corners too sharp. But he displayed patience and determination in each try.

When the shape finally held, she dipped a finger in moonwater and then brushed it along its base, weaving a quiet pulse of golden magic into the paper. The lantern glowed, soft as a held breath.

Their hands brushed.
Neither moved away.

By twilight, a basket of finished lanterns hung from Thessa's arm as they walked the narrow path to the beach. Evran stayed close beside her, not touching, but close enough she could feel his heat.

The tide was low, leaving ripples in the sand like threads pulled across fabric. They set the lanterns gently in the shallows, watching as the first flames caught the reflection of the rising moon.

One by one, small lights drifted outward, silver and gold on the darkening water — like memories being released, like blessings being carried.

Thessa whispered the words of blessings her father had taught her, her voice barely louder than the breeze. "For memory. For peace. For the ones still waiting to be found."

Evran added his own, voice roughened by something tender. "For those learning to live again."

They watched until the last lantern disappeared into the dark horizon.

As they turned back towards the cottage, the lighthouse beam bathed them in its warmth. Evran reached for her hand — tentative, almost questioning.

Thessa let her fingers twine with his.

They walked in silence up the path, fingers still twined, the echo of folded paper and candleflame lingering between them like a shared heartbeat. The cottage waited ahead, warm light spilling through the windows. Thessa was halfway to the door when Evran's hand tightened around hers.

"Thessa — wait."

She turned. His chest rose and fell too quickly, like courage gathering itself. Moonlight touched the side of his face, softening the fear in his eyes but not hiding it.

"I was going to leave in the morning," he said. "Before I said anything foolish. Before I… hoped for more than I should."

Her breath hitched, sharp and small.

He stepped closer. "But tonight, folding those boats with you… sending them out together. I realized something." His voice roughened. "I don't want to go."

Wind caught the hem of his shirt. He didn't seem to notice.

"I love you," he said plainly. As if he'd held it for so long he could not shape it into anything else. "I love how you listen to the sea like it speaks a language only you hear. How you care for people even when you're hurting. How you meet the world with courage even when your body betrays you." He swallowed hard. "I love how you look at me like I'm someone worth staying for."

Her heart thudded once, deep and loud.

His voice dropped to something almost unsteady. "I love you, Thessa Fenwyck. And if you'll have me, if you want me…I want my life to be here. With you."

For a moment she couldn't speak. All the years of loneliness, of being seen only as frail or broken or useful, rose in her throat like a tide.

And then they broke.

She stepped into him, pressing her forehead to his. "I love you," she whispered. "I love the man who ran toward fire even when it broke him. The man who fixed my roof and then stayed to help mend my heart. The man who looks at me and sees all of me. Not just my magic. Not just my illness. Me."

His breath shook.

"And yes," she said, slipping her hands up the front of his shirt. "Stay. Please stay."

Relief crashed through his smile like sunlight through storm clouds, and he pressed a light kiss to her lips.

She tangled her fingers in his and pulled him toward the door. "Come inside," she murmured.

Evran laughed. Soft, disbelieving, full of joy, and followed her over the threshold.

The door closed behind them with a quiet, certain click.

EPILOGUE

EVRAN

The sea was calm that morning. The kind of stillness that only came after years of learning how to listen.

Evran crouched near the shoreline, the sand cool and damp beneath his boots. A square of paper rested in his hands. He folded it carefully along the creases, guiding smaller fingers through the motions beside him.

"That's it," he murmured, smiling as his son's brow furrowed with fierce concentration. "Sharp fold here... then bring the corners to the middle."

The boy's tongue poked out in determined focus, a mirror of Thessa when she worked. "Like this, Papa?"

"Exactly like that."

They pressed the final crease together, and the child's delighted laugh lifted into the morning air when the little boat took shape. Evran held it up toward the soft dawn light. "Your first one. Your mother will be proud."

"She already is," Thessa said from behind them.

She stood at the edge of the path, a shawl wrapped around her shoulders, her hair catching the glow of sunrise. Bits of silver had just started to wind through it, fine as starlight, beautiful as truth. "You've done well, both of you."

Evran's chest warmed, a place that had once held only ache now full of something gentler. "We thought we might send this one out for Rion."

Thessa stepped closer, her expression tender, and pressed a kiss to the top of their son's head. "A good morning for it."

The boy glanced up at them, uncertain. "Who's Rion?"

Evran knelt again, placing the small boat in his son's hands. "He was my best friend. He loved the sea as much as you do."

"Did he go away?" the child asked.

Evran nodded. "He did. A long time ago. But he's still part of me and of the sea. Part of every wave, every nail I hammer, every boat we fold together."

The boy considered this, serious and thoughtful, then whispered, "Then he'll see it, won't he?"

"Yes," Evran said quietly. "He'll see it."

They walked together to the edge of the tide. Morning sunlight spilled across the water, turning each ripple to gold. Evran steadied his son's hand as they set the paper boat gently on the surface. The first wave caught it, carrying it outward.

The boat bobbed once, twice, then caught the current. Light rippled over it, gold and white, until it was just a flicker against the bright sea.

Evran's chest tightened. Not with sorrow. It was something warmer, quieter. A kind of love that had found its peace.

He glanced at Thessa. She was watching him with the kind of love and knowing that came from years of building a life together. "He'd be proud of you," she said.

Evran exhaled, the breeze carrying his answer out to sea. "I hope so. But I think… I'm proud of me, too."

Their son squealed as the next wave chased his feet up the sand, laughter echoing through the morning air.

Evran reached for Thessa's hand, twining his fingers through hers. The sea shimmered. The horizon glowed with promise.

They stood together — the keeper and the craftsman, the light and the tide — watching a small paper boat drift toward open water as their son played in the waves.

And somewhere out in that vast sweep of gold and blue, Evran could almost hear a familiar voice carried on the wind — warm, teasing, alive.

About time, old friend.

He smiled, letting the words settle over him like sunlight.

Then he turned and walked with his little family toward the lighthouse, toward the home they had built, and back to the life waiting within its walls.

Acknowledgements

I want to take a minute to thank the people in my life that have taken my pain seriously but still treat me as a worthwhile person. It's easy to feel like you don't quite fit in when you suffer from chronic pain. A lot of people don't understand the strength it can take to just get out of bed and do the things you must and instead view you as either weak or someone who just complains a lot.

Thank you to my family. You provide me with endless support, challenges, and love. My relationships with you are what make life worthwhile.

Thank you to my amazing beta readers. It takes special people to be willing to read my unpolished messes and see my vision. Thank you for helping shape my stories.

To My Readers

I hope you've enjoyed the story of Evran and Thessa's romance. It means a lot that you take time from your lives to read the story that's been swimming in my head for months.

Thessa shows symptoms of rheumatoid arthritis. RA is an autoimmune condition where the body starts attacking its own tissue. Often this is seen in the joints with pain, stiffness, and inflammation, but it can also attack other parts of the body such as the heart. If you suspect you may have RA please consult your medical professional. You are not weak for seeking help with you pain, it takes strength to admit you need help!

If you enjoy my storytelling style please check out my first novel ThreadWoven, the first book in a trilogy called The ThreadCrafted Series. The second book is planned for release in the Spring of 2026.

You can find me on Facebook as Brynne Aisling-Rowan Author, on Instagram @authorbrynneaislingrowan, or join my story circle at www.wovenmoonpress.com for news and exclusive content.

About the Author

Brynne Aisling-Rowan writes romance and cozy fantasy rooted in quiet magic, crafted worlds, and the emotional threads that bind people together. Her stories blend cozy atmosphere with grief, hope, and the soft resilience found in handmade things. When she isn't writing about lighthouses, paper spells, or characters learning how to carry their sorrows, she's crocheting, gathering yarn like a dragon hoards treasure, or drinking tea from mugs large enough to be mildly impractical.

She lives in the Midwest with her husband, two adult sons, and two very opinionated canine beasts who remain convinced they are her creative directors.

Papercraft is her second novel.